THE CISCO KID
IN THE BRONX
Episodes in the Life of a Young Man

Miguel Antonio Ortiz

Hamilton Stone Editions
Maplewood, New Jersey

Cover design by Adalberto Ortiz
Many thanks to Meredith Sue Willis
for encouraging the publication of this book.

Acknowledgements: "The Coat" appeared in *The Point: Where Teaching and Writing Intersect*, a Teachers & Writers Collaborative anthology. "Lola" appeared in *Confrontation,* Long Island University magazine. "The Installments Man" appeared in *Hanging Together, Hanging Loose Press 20th Anniversary Anthology.*

Library of Congress Cataloging-in-Publication Data

Ortiz, Miguel Antonio, 1944–
  The Cisco Kid in the Bronx / by Miguel Antonio Ortiz.
    p. cm.
  ISBN 978-0-9801786-9-2 (alk. paper)
  1. Puerto Ricans—New York (State)—New York—Fiction. 2. Immigrants—New York (State)—New York—Fiction. 3. Bronx (New York, N.Y.)—Fiction. I. Title.
  PS3615.R825C57 2012
  813'.6–dc22
                        2011024240

Contents

The River

*I*T RAINED ALL day and all night the way it must have rained the forty days and forty nights that flooded the Earth. The clay ground bled, and my feet grew red as I ran barefoot bathing in the blood of the Earth, warm as dragon's blood.

"The river will flood. The bridge will wash away," Grandfather said.

"Maybe it will stop raining soon," Father said.

"Not today," Grandfather said.

He had built the bridge. He and the river were old enemies.

By the afternoon of the next day, the rain stopped. To get home, we had to cross the river. On the road through the cane fields, it was a short distance to the bridge. From the crest of the hill, we saw the river wind until it disappeared in the tall grass. Usually, the water was as green as the grass, but now the water was yellow. The bridge was still there, water flowing over it very fast.

"We can cross," Father said.

"We don't have to. We can go the long way," Mother said.

"We can cross," he insisted. "The bridge is still there."

By the bridge we heard the logs knocking against each other.

"I will take Mario across first," Father said. There were two logs left and they were loose. "Hold on to my hand," Father said.

We sidestepped onto the bridge—one hand on the railing, one hand in each other's. The logs moved under our feet. The opaque yellowness lapped about our ankles like so many tongues.

A log rolled and I rolled with it. Father held tight to my hand and pulled me up. One foot felt heavier than the other.

"He lost his shoe," Mother shouted from the bank.

Father and I moved back to where she stood. He began to undress.

"Leave it," Mother pleaded. "Leave it, for God's sake!"

Father dove into the river. Downstream from the bridge, he came out shoe in hand. He walked back to where Mother and I waited.

"You tempt God," Mother said.

"We'll go the long way," he said as he handed me the shoe.

Rogers Place

The Coat

WHEN IT SNOWED, my brother and I watched from our window. Roofs, antennas, skylights all turned white.

"I don't want to go out by myself," Pedrito said.

"You have to. We can't both go. I'll watch you from here." Mother was in the other room ironing. "Ma!" I shouted. "Can Pedrito go out in the snow, then me?"

"All right," she said. "But don't cross the street."

We had arrived in October before the cold weather had set in. My father, who had been here for six months, met us at the airport. He had light jackets for us, okay for the autumn. When winter came, we got an old coat from a cousin whom we had never met before. Then we had one coat, but there were two of us.

Pedrito put on the coat. It had a checkered pattern running from the shoulders to the waist on either sides of the front. He went out to the street.

From the window, I watched and waited for him to appear in the empty lot next to the building. Falling snow was piling up on the window ledge. I opened the window a little, gathered the white powder into a ball and tossed it from hand to hand. My fingers became red, so I rested the ball on the windowsill. I looked out on the white world. It was silent, everything numb.

Pedrito appeared in the lot. He raised his hands over his head and waved, then he shouted something, but I couldn't hear him. He ran around, twice stopping to shake the snow from his shoes. He made a snowball and threw it against the brick wall. Then he disappeared around the edge of the building.

Soon he was back.

"It's too cold," he said. "My feet are freezing."

"I got some snow from the ledge," I said. I turned to get the snowball. There was a puddle on the windowsill and water dripping to the floor.

"You better clean it up," he said, glancing toward the other room.

I got the dishrag from the sink and was wiping up the water when my mother walked in. She didn't say anything. I waited.

"How's the snow?" she asked Pedrito.

"Too cold," he said. "My feet got wet."

"Put on a dry pair of socks," she told him. She sat him down on a chair and took off his shoes and socks. She rubbed his feet to make them warm.

"Are you going out too, Mario?" she asked.

"Yeah, I want to see what it's like."

"It's cold!" Pedrito said.

"Get something from the store," she said. She didn't say anything about the water dripping from the windowsill. She told me what to get. Pedrito handed me the coat.

"Here's the notebook," Mother said.

I reached out for the little notebook and put it in the coat pocket.

Under the battered mailboxes in the hallway, the radiator knocked loudly as I hurried into the street. My brother's footprints were almost gone, covered by falling snow. The only one out in the street, I stood still on the stoop wondering what to do. I looked up to let the snow fall on my face. Snowflakes melted on my nose and cheeks. I made a snowball and threw it at a parked car, then looked around to check whether anyone had seen me.

I ran a little on the sidewalk then looked back to see my tracks. I walked backward stepping in my footprints. It looked as if I had disappeared where my tracks stopped. That was an Indian trick I had seen in a comic book. I had seen a lot of things in comic books, especially in comic books about Indians.

Suppose an Indian wanted a coat. He'd go out in the woods, hunt down a bear, take the skin, and make himself a bearskin coat. First he'd look for tracks, then dig a hole right on the tracks because that's where the bear walks. He'd cover the hole with branches so that it'd looks like there's no hole there at all. When the bear comes by, swapo! Right into the trap.

I wished I could hunt down a bear for a coat. I went into the empty lot, and I started to dig a hole in the snow. I knew there weren't any bears in the Bronx, but there was nothing else to do. I looked up and saw Pedrito at the window.

Pointing at the hole, I shouted up to him, "I'm gonna catch a bear!"

He put his hand to his ear. I shouted louder. He shook his head, his hand still at his ear. I wished that he were helping me dig the hole. But then, if he were with me, there wouldn't be any need to catch a bear. I got to thinking that since there were no bears, probably the only thing that would fall in the hole would be a stray dog. That wouldn't be any good for a coat.

Digging a hole in the snow was hard work. With no gloves and no galoshes, I couldn't tell whether my hands were colder than my feet. The wind started up, and the snowflakes went wild, running in waves trying to escape but only dashing themselves against cars and walls, then falling unconscious to the ground. Trying to warm my hands in the coat pockets, I found the little notebook. I went to the grocery store.

A little bell in the back was attached to the door by a string. Whenever the door opened, the bell rang to let Don Justino, the grocer, know that someone was in. That way, if anybody came to rob him, he wouldn't be caught by surprise. He also had a German shepherd that growled all the time. It had attacked him once. Don Justino had bandages all over his face and hands, but he still kept the dog. I guess he was more afraid of losing his money, though he did put a muzzle on the dog after that.

In addition to the store, Don Justino owned a brick house and behind the house a row of garages that he rented out. Everyone bought on credit at Don Justino's. He even lent out money. He was always writing down numbers. He wrote in his big book how much you owed him; then he wrote the amount in your little book. Sometimes people just said a number to him, and he wrote it down in a different book.

11

On Sundays, he gave money to policemen. That was, my father said, so that he might sell beer on a day meant for going to church.

The bell rang when I walked into the store. Some of the snow tried to get in with me.

"*Dos libras de arroz y una caja de habichuelas,*" I said to Don Justino.

Grinning like fat little men, candy jars sat on the counter. The jellybean jar laughed a rainbow of jellybean colors that broke up into perfect jellybeans. The more it laughed the more jellybeans appeared. Then they fell on the counter making a sound like raindrops on a windowpane.

"Anything else?" Don Justino asked.

The jellybeans disappeared.

I handed him the little notebook. He wrote down how much we owed him for the rice and beans. Another kid walked in with a notebook just like mine.

"Isn't that your brother's coat?" he asked.

I didn't answer, but he went on, "You wanna come out later to play?"

"I don't know," I said. "My name is Mario. My brother's name is Pedrito."

"I'm Raymond. Your brother can't come. He don't have no coat."

I didn't say nothing.

The Cisco Kid in the Bronx

*I*N THE BRONX there is a valley along the bottom of which runs a street called Rogers Place. A segment of that street is bordered at one end by Westchester Avenue and the elevated IRT that runs up to White Plains Road. On a slope at the other end, Horseshoe Park descends, the curve of the horseshoe a downward incline. The park interrupts 163rd Street; steps lead down the hill, then 163rd Street resumes. Rogers Place ends at the park. A pathway through the park leads to another street, the way to Public School 99. On Rogers Place, the street that runs through the valley and ends at Horseshoe Park, lived for some years the Cisco Kid.

He spoke English just like the gringos, and he could shoot his six-shooter over his shoulder so that the bullet would ricochet on the front pillars of 957 Rogers Place and hit the bad guy right between the eyes, or in the stomach, or just hit him on the hand to knock his weapon to the ground.

The Kid came down in the morning from his fifth-floor apartment. He unhitched his black horse, Diablo, that had been standing all night by the iron railing in front of the building. As the Kid put his spurred black boot in the stirrup and pulled himself up, swinging one leg over the croup of his horse, the round silver medallions that ran down the side of his trousers caught the sunlight and for a split second reflected every which way.

The people of the valley had entrusted the Kid with a job that nobody else wanted. They expected him to live up to it, and he took it seriously. The Kid rode up to Horseshoe Park. Diablo, an agile horse, leaped up the steps. From the top of the hill the Kid saw every movement in the park.

Strangers were unwelcome. The people of the valley, especially Don Justino, the grocer, had enough of strangers. Strangers might be undercover cops investigating the numbers. Don Alfonso, who lived on the first floor of 759 Rogers Place, the very same building the Kid made his home, was involved with the numbers also. The Kid had placed a number with him once. Not a gambler at heart, he did it out of sheer impulse.

He had been standing on the stoop of the building, a silver coin burning a hole in his pocket. The world seemed dull to the Kid that day. He felt trapped in the valley. He would have liked to jump on Diablo and ride away, never to come back, but that was impossible. He had a responsibility—he had to stay. He put his hand in his pocket and held the coin tightly in the palm of his hand.

He wasn't wearing his black silver-trimmed outfit that day. In his everyday clothes, no one could tell him apart from an ordinary citizen. The Kid often pondered why people didn't recognize him when he was dressed in his regular clothes. He concluded that that was the nature of humanity. He wasn't the only hero who was unrecognizable without his costume. There wasn't much point in ruminating about such things.

There he was with a silver coin in his pocket and a dull world staring him in the face. Maybe if he hit a number, he would feel better, a novel thought for the Kid. He wasn't sure that it was proper for someone in his position to gamble. But after all, everyone did. It was part of life—*la vida*, as they say in those parts. The Kid turned from the sun-bathed stoop and walked into the gaping vestibule of the building. The churning of his stomach, an unusual sensation for him, troubled him as he knocked on the door of Don Alfonso's apartment.

Don Alfonso appeared wearing his usual white shirt. At home, he didn't sport the jacket of his pinstripe suit. His hair slicked back on a head that seemed too small for his body, he overshadowed the Kid.

"I want to put a dime on 456," the Kid said extending his hand toward the big man.

Don Alfonso took the coin, placed it in his own pocket and closed the door in the Kid's face.

The Kid stood there knowing something had happened but not

14

quite understanding what, the feeling similar to discovering oneself still on the sidewalk after having the definite impression of having climbed into the bus. He had expected Don Alfonso to put the dime in some special place. Perhaps Don Alfonso should have invited him in, shaken his hand, offered him some refreshment, talked about the weather, perhaps. After all, the Kid had made an overture of friendship and trust; surely, recognition of that was in order.

However, since it wasn't forthcoming, the Kid took it philosophically. Perhaps Don Alfonso had a photographic memory. Maybe he didn't need to note down his customers; but more likely, the dime was gone forever into the fathomless darkness of Don Alfonso's pocket. Don Alfonso would have no memory of the transaction. He didn't look at faces and, on that day, the Kid wasn't wearing the black silver-trimmed clothes that would have made him immediately identifiable.

The Kid knew that it was his own fault that Don Alfonso didn't recognize him, so he let it go. He walked back into the sunlight and continued about his business incognito.

Lola

I DREAMT THAT my father owned the Third Avenue El, the part that ran in the Bronx. The downtown segment had already been torn down. He stood by the turnstiles, and anybody he didn't like, he didn't let on the train. Aunt Lola came up to him and demanded payment of all the money he owed her. He said he couldn't pay till he got to the end of the line. So he and Aunt Lola got on the train and rode to the end of the line in the middle of a park. There was a goat there tied to a tree. My father untied the goat and gave it to Lola. I shouted, "It's my goat. It's my goat." But nobody paid any attention to me. Aunt Lola walked away with the goat. Nothing terrible happened in the dream, but the mood of it was scary, like a horror movie, only worse.

I had a goat once, a long time ago when I was a child in Puerto Rico. We had relatives who lived in the mountains. Once, when we went to visit them, they gave me a baby goat. She was a nice little goat with black spots. We put her in a box, and my father carried her down the mountain to town, where we boarded a public car to go home to Bayamon.

My father worked at a hospital. He had an office all to himself with a large desk and a typewriter. Behind his desk there was a window that let in the sunlight. In one corner of the room hung a skeleton that on Halloween he brought home to hang on our porch. The hospital owned a great deal of land and provided housing for some of its employees. Right behind the hospital there was housing for visiting doctors. Our house was farther away, across the pasture where the hospital cattle grazed.

Right in front of our house, so she could eat as much grass as she wanted, I tied the little goat with a long rope. That very first day, she got loose and ran across the pasture toward the hospital. My father ran

16

after the goat, and my mother ran after him, and I ran after the three of them.

It was fun chasing the goat across the pasture, but I was afraid that she might fall into the ditch by the road. When she stopped, my father bent down to pick up the end of the rope. She started to run again, and my father lost his balance. He fell right into cow dung. He got it all over his shirt. My mother couldn't stop laughing though she was the one who had to wash and iron the shirt.

Morivivir, a thorny plant that grows close to the ground, has leaves that look like pine needles. When you touch the plant, all the leaves fold up close to the stem and the thorns show. In a little while, it opens up again. I took the goat for a walk, and when I wasn't looking she began to eat morivivir. As soon as I noticed, I dragged her away, but it was too late. She had eaten the thorns. I thought they would rip up her stomach, and she would die. On my way home, I cried because my goat would die, and it was my fault.

When I told my mother why I was crying, she laughed. "Silly, thorns don't bother goats. They can eat anything."

I didn't know whether or not to believe her. I stopped crying and waited for the goat to die, but she survived.

Every first Tuesday of the month, all the cows belonging to the hospital were herded down the road to the big ranch where they plunged into a vat filled with chemicals to get rid of anything harmful on their skin. When the goat was old enough, my grandfather, Don Francisco, and I drove her along with the cows to the big ranch, and she waded through the vat also.

The ditch had a fence on each side to keep the animals in line. I stood by the fence watching as the cows went in one by one. A man with a long stick and a can of paint stood on the other side of the vat. He marked each cow as it went by.

"He can't poke my goat. She'll be hurt," I said to my grandfather.

"It doesn't hurt," he said.

Afterward, when the paint had dried, I felt the patch, the little goat's hair all stuck together.

Grandfather knew a lot about goats and about other animals too. One day he said we should get the goat mated. So we took her to a place, not far away, where they had a billy goat. We left the two goats together in a small pasture. The billy goat had a brown body, almost red. My grandfather and I sat a little ways away on the side of a hill. We talked about life in general and about goats too.

I don't remember much about my grandfather except that he was nice to me, and he taught me to take care of animals. I never saw him again after I came to America.

When we moved to New York, Lola came with us.

"Are you sure you want to do this?" my mother asked her. Lola was her younger sister. "You can't live with us. The apartment Juan has for us is too small."

"It's all right," Lola said. "I'm not staying in New York. I have a friend in Chicago. I'm going there to stay with her."

Mother wasn't thrilled to have Lola travel with us, better if Lola arrived in New York on her own. But my mother couldn't stop her. She couldn't say to her own sister, "Lola, you can't travel with us." What did it matter anyway if she did? She would be off to Chicago; wherever that was in North America, it couldn't be too far from New York.

My father had come to New York first. Found a job, dishwasher in a cafeteria, and an apartment; then, he sent for us. The apartment, a fifth-floor walk-up, had three small rooms. When we got off the plane, we were all glad to see each other. Father acted happy even to see Lola, but we knew he wasn't. Mother had been worried all along about how he would react. I could see how glad she was that he didn't say anything about Lola right away. I guess she kept hoping that Lola's story about going to Chicago would be true. But deep down she was afraid that it wasn't, and she was right. Lola moved in with us into the three-room apartment in the Bronx.

Like a child, Lola was never sure of herself, and she never took charge of anything. Sometimes Mother got angry with her because she let my brother, Pedrito, and me do anything we wanted. Then Lola would say, "They're not my children. I can't tell them what to do. They don't listen to me anyway."

"You're an adult, act like one," my mother snapped. "If you act like an adult, they'll listen to you."

Lola looked at my mother in disbelief. She was sure that nothing she said would make any difference. I think she was right. It was hard to take Lola seriously. She seemed always to be cringing as if some heavy object, the sky maybe, was just about to fall on her. Pedrito said to me, "Doesn't Lola look like she's always tiptoeing when she walks?" We thought it was funny, another of her odd ways. She was stoop shouldered, too. She stooped and tiptoed through her life hoping that misfortune wouldn't notice her.

Lola was always afraid, but sometimes she was too stubborn to get out of the way of trouble. Back in Bayamon, from the porch of our house by the pasture, we had once watched Lola trying to learn how to ride a bicycle. A friend of hers held the bicycle straight until Lola could pedal away. It was funny—a grown person trying to learn something children could do.

"Why do you waste your time on that?" my mother asked. She had never been on a bicycle.

Lola had walked in straight and excited, but on hearing Mother's words, she went back to her usual posture. "I don't know why. I just want to, for fun," she said.

"Do whatever you want," my mother said, "but people will talk."

"Let them say what they want. Talk isn't going to kill me."

"What does Enrique think of it?" Mother asked.

Enrique was Lola's boyfriend. He found out about the bicycle soon enough, and he didn't like it one bit. He gave Lola a choice, either him or the bicycle.

"Why did you have to tell him?" my mother asked. "Don't you have any sense?"

"I didn't tell him," said Lola. "Maybe he saw me."

"He didn't have to see you. People talk," Mother said.

"If I want to ride a bicycle, he's not going to stop me. There are plenty of fish in the ocean," Lola responded. So she made her choice. It wasn't Enrique, and it wasn't the bicycle either.

In New York, she didn't know how to get around. Besides, she couldn't speak English. She sat in the house looking miserable and doing nothing unless she was told. At night, unpleasant things happened, and everyone would go to bed in a bad mood.

Mother and Father had arguments about money.

"How am I going to feed this family?" Mother would ask. "How am I going to feed them? We owe so much. I'm ashamed to keep shopping on credit. You promised you would pay the grocer two weeks ago. What do you do with money? It slips away like water through your fingers."

She wept. He got angry.

Lilian cried also. She was the youngest, and she cried for almost anything. Still a baby, she slept in the same room with Mother and Father. Pedrito and me slept in the other room, and we pretended we didn't hear anything. Lola slept in the kitchen in a fold-up bed. In the morning, she folded it, and covered it with a blanket tucked in around the edges so that it looked neat. She then pushed it against the wall. The kitchen doubled as living room; when we had company, the bed was opened to sit on.

The kitchen was the center of the apartment. You had to walk through it to get to the bathroom. Lola slept with every bit of her under the blankets so that she would not be seen by anyone going to the bathroom at night. She slept on her back with the blanket pulled over her face. She looked stiff like a mummy.

On her face, she used a pimple cream that stunk up the kitchen every night. The black cream looked like axle grease but made the room smell like a hospital. Sometimes, she put rubber ringlets in her hair and tied a handkerchief over her head. Then, she put on the black cream. She was a sight. We nicknamed her "Miss America."

We went to bed early, and we had to put out the light to save on electricity. Me and my brother always kept talking in bed after the lights were out. Sometimes we talked for a long time, and sometimes we giggled and laughed, and we couldn't stop. Maybe we made noise so we wouldn't have to worry about the darkness. I was afraid of the dark. I would always see shapes of monsters creeping around in it. I think Pedrito was afraid too, but he didn't admit it. Anyway, Lola didn't like the noise we made. It kept her awake, she said. There was no door between our room and the kitchen, so it was almost like being in the same room.

"Shush," she hissed at us.

"Shush yourself," I answered.

We were quiet for a few minutes, then we started to talk again.

"Be quiet in there," Lola hissed.

"We are quiet."

"If you don't stop, I'm going to tell your mother."

From her room, Mother heard everything anyway. "Now go to sleep, all of you," she admonished.

In a little while Pedrito got up to go to the bathroom. On his way, he turned on the light in the kitchen, and Lola began complaining again.

"What's going on out there?" Mother asked at the top of her voice.

"I have to go to the bathroom."

"He doesn't have to go. All he wants is to bother me," Lola said.

"I don't want to have to get up," Mother threatened.

Usually after that, we kept quiet and fell asleep but not always. Then, Mother would get up and scream at us. It was all Lola's fault. We wished she wasn't there sleeping in the kitchen like a mummy all covered with her pimple cream. Pedrito and me, we tried to ignore her as much as possible. Sometimes, though, a big fight would break out

21

over nothing, like the time Pedrito left a bunch of crayons in the middle of the floor, and Lola moved them, so she wouldn't step on them. He started shouting and carrying on, and she shouted and screamed back at him.

I don't know if Lola ever had any fun except when she went to church. She joined Las Hijas de Maria, a church group for girls. They wore white dresses when they went to mass. They had meetings too, and sometimes they had dances, but Lola never did any dancing. That wasn't important to her, or so she said. She liked wearing the white dress, and marching in processions, and taking trips to holy shrines, and on holydays singing in the church while sitting up front with the group.

Whenever anyone, mostly Aunt Luisa, my father's sister, said anything to Lola about her trying to find a man and getting married, Lola would say that she didn't want to get married because then she wouldn't be allowed to be in the Daughters of Mary. You had to be a virgin to belong; so when the girls got married, they couldn't be in it anymore. I think all the other girls wanted more to get married than to be Daughters of Mary, but Lola was different.

She tried working in garment factories, but the work was never steady. She would work a few weeks then be laid off. Finally, she got into domestic work. On the first day of her last job as a maid, her employer came to pick her up. Very tall and as pale as white putty, he was very nervous when he walked into our apartment. He didn't sit down, just said hello and picked up her suitcase and carried it down to his car. He was a lawyer, and he had a wife and two daughters.

Lola had a room in their house all to herself with her own television. Every other weekend, she came home to stay with us. The work was all right, she said, but the children didn't pay her any mind, just like Pedrito and me. She worked there a few months, then she cracked up. She went batty, and she had to be sent to a state hospital.

She was in the hospital for a while. At first, Mother was very upset. "I did my best," she said. "It's not my fault. Lola was never the same after Mama died. I was only fourteen. I did the best I could." She said that every time anybody talked about Lola.

When they let Lola out, she still had to go to the outpatient clinic, and she had to take pills. They told her not to work; that would be too much for her. So she had to be on welfare. But she didn't want to stay home and do nothing.

"What am I going to do here?" she asked. "I'm so bored, and this little bit of money I get is not enough."

"If you work, they'll take that money away. You'll lose your job, and you'll have nothing," my mother warned her.

"Nah, I'll do it secretly."

So, again she worked in factories. She'd lose one job and find another. Since her illness, she hadn't changed much, except that she smoked cigarettes, and her stubbornness came out more often. Sometimes she sat a long time staring out the window, and she would start to cry. Nobody could figure out why she was crying; there was nothing to see from that window but a little bit of the street and some roofs. That's all. Anyway, she didn't cry much, just for a little while, then she would stop.

Lola met a man who asked her out. It was an event because everyone had given up hope that any man would be interested in her. The man came to our place to meet my mother. He wore a brown suit, a vest, and very polished shoes. His hair was greased and combed back close to his head, every single strand in place. He had a little moustache too. He had terrific manners, and he talked very nicely.

Mother was very impressed with how nice he was. To me, his long face and moustache made him look like a mouse—a mouse all dressed up in a suit. I could just see him scurrying across the floor and into a crack in the wall. He wanted to take Lola to a dance, and my mother said it was all right. Lola was very happy ironing the dress and the petticoat she was going to wear.

She didn't come home that night. Mother was going out of her mind trying to figure out where Lola could be. She went looking for her, but there was no trace. Lola came back late the next day, her dress torn and her face bruised. She had gone to the man's apartment, and he had tried to force her. She had fought him off, she said. My mother didn't know what do with herself. She couldn't help being furious at Lola, but she didn't want to make her feel worse.

Lola gave the police a couple of days to catch the criminal. When they didn't, she went after him herself. There was nothing anyone could say to stop her. She waited in hiding until the man came back to the apartment, then she called Detective Patrick, who had been assigned to the case. He made the arrest. My mother and Lola testified at the trial.

"I think they beat him up," my mother said when they came home. "There was blood all over his shirt. They shouldn't have done that."

"They didn't beat him enough," Father said.

"No, it's not right. The police are not supposed to do that." My mother felt sorry for everyone. She couldn't see any suffering without feeling pity.

Detective Patrick came to the house after the trial. He talked to Lola, and he seemed very sincere and sorry about her problem. He had very blue eyes, and he looked like he was always ready to tell a joke. My mother put ten dollars in an envelope and told me to give it to him. I handed him the envelope. I thought he would refuse it, but he didn't. He put it in his pocket. In those days, I didn't know much about cops.

Lola was in the welfare office the second time she cracked up. For hours, she had been waiting there, in a big room with a high ceiling. She had to listen very carefully for her name to be called. It was hard to hear in that room. There were rows and rows of folding chairs with people sitting in them. Lola began to talk to herself, but no one noticed her. Still talking, she paced up and down the aisle. Nobody noticed anything unusual about her until she began to violently bang a chair on a desk.

Mother visited Lola in the hospital regularly even though it was a long trip. She would get somebody to drive—sometimes one of my uncles and sometimes just an acquaintance. She always gave the person ten dollars for the gas.

For a long time Lola didn't speak to anyone. She just sat on her bed, her hair uncombed, wearing only the hospital smock. She refused to wear any of her own clothes. If they gave them to her, she tore them up. She didn't eat anything either. She thought the devil was in the food and if she ate, he would get inside of her.

My father never liked going to see Lola even when she got better. He would just as well have left her in the hospital and forgotten about her, but Mother nagged him, so he went to see Lola sometimes. Mother said Lola asked about me. I felt bad because I didn't like to go up to the hospital either. It was a long trip, and I didn't have anything to say to Lola anyway.

Sometimes, we all went and pretended we were going to a picnic out in the country. It was a long drive up the Saw Mill River Parkway. I had not seen so many trees and woods since I came to New York. Lola came down to be with us on the hospital lawn.

I asked Lola how she was.

She said, "Fine."

She asked me how things were with me.

I said, "Okay."

She never stayed with us too long before going back to the ward.

On the way back, we stopped to rest by the roadside. A stream flowed down out of the woods. It was very pretty. Across the road, over a field, there was a house and near it an old pickup truck that maybe didn't run anymore. On a long rope, a billy goat was tied to the front bumper of the truck. I looked at the goat for a long time. It reminded me of the goat I once had.

My goat had two kids. So I had three goats, the mother and two little ones. One day my father sold all three of them. He sold them to Fernando, the doctor's son, who was having a party. "He wanted to serve goat fricassee," my father said standing by the door of our house when he came back from the party.

They must've tied the goat's legs then cut her throat. They must have hung her from her hind legs to let the blood drain out, a tin tub under her to catch the blood. That's the way animals are killed for eating. I didn't know whether they killed the two little goats for that fricassee or whether they kept them to kill them when they grew up. My father got paid for the goats, but I never saw any of the money, not even a penny. That's the way my father is sometimes. If you have no power to stop him, he does what he wants. I don't know how he got to be that way.

All the way home from the state hospital, I thought about the goat and about my grandfather, who taught me how to take care of animals and whom I never saw again after I came to America.

The Installments Man

MR. CARLTON LOOKED tired as he approached Intervale Avenue. He didn't relish the prospect of climbing another five flights of stairs to where every Thursday evening the necessity of his business brought him. He looked at his watch; he was right on time. He believed punctuality to be of utmost importance. He thought it provided comfort to his clients, and he expected them, in return, to reciprocate by not falling in arrears. He was often disappointed, but he took solace in the knowledge that it was not due to his negligence that others failed to carry out their rightful obligations.

The narrow stairway made him aware of his own size. He reflected on what it meant to be a fat man. For indeed, he could not deny to himself that he was overweight; he attempted to take it in stride. He had no illusions about his appearance. Or rather, he had no fantasies about looking otherwise than he did. He occasionally experienced a bout of anxiety about his health but not often enough to induce him to change his habits. He arrived at the fifth floor somewhat out of breath. He knocked on the door and waited for the inevitable question.

It seemed to him a long time before he heard a woman's voice ask, "Who is it?"

"Carlton," he answered. He tried to sound authoritative, but his weariness took the edge off his voice.

He wished that he were somewhere else—in Miami staying at a hotel where he would be waited on hand and foot. By this time, he would have been in a restaurant having a drink before dinner. His brother, who lived in Miami, had always been the lucky one—the one to whom everything came easily, the one who didn't have to climb tenement stairs to wring a bit of money out of people in miserable circumstances.

He heard the turning of the lock, and the door opened just enough to reveal the puzzled face of the woman. She wasn't pleased to see him. They were never pleased to see him, though they were pleased enough to come down to the store to buy on credit.

"Already?" escaped from the woman's mouth. She seemed surprised to hear her own utterance as if it had produced itself involuntarily.

"It's Thursday," Carlton assured her wishing that she were more pleasant, that they were all more pleasant. Their tense faces made him feel awkward.

The door ajar, Mrs. Ortega stood there as if she didn't know what to do next, the routine forgotten. She was supposed to go to the cupboard that stood by her kitchen door, and from a pile of paper that lay there, she was supposed to pull the payment book that usually contained five dollars. She would hand the book and the money to Carlton, who would put the money in his pocket, write down the amount in the book and on his own record card and hand the book back to Mrs. Ortega. Sometimes, there would be no money; one of the children would say, "He didn't leave anything today." Meaning that Mr. Ortega was neglecting to make a payment. Mr. Ortega was seldom home when Carlton came by.

Mrs. Ortega remained silent. She didn't move from the door but merely looked at him as if she had forgotten her lines. He had to improvise or prompt her without making a fuss. He was not cut out for this sort of thing. Some people always knew what to say, made any situation seem funny and were loved for that, but not Georgie Carlton.

"Are you all right, Mr. Carlton?" Mrs. Ortega asked.

Of course, I'm all right, he thought, just a little out of breath from climbing the stairs. He was perspiring a great deal. He reached into his pocket and pulled out his handkerchief to wipe his brow. The damn stairs were too steep. Debtors ought to live in buildings with elevators.

"You better come in and sit down," she said.

For a moment, the unexpected civility perplexed him. "No, I'm all right," he said, but his knees felt weak. He made an effort to remain on his feet.

"Come in," she repeated grabbing him by the arm. "Juan!" she called, "Juan!" She was a slight woman. The contrast of his great bulk being assisted by so frail a person made him feel more vulnerable. Mr. Ortega emerged from the rear of the apartment, but Carlton had already eased himself into the first available piece of furniture, one of the chairs at the kitchen table.

From there, Carlton looked into the living room where a child was trying to escape his gaze by peering from behind an armchair. All the children in this family seemed extremely shy. The older ones, out of sight at the moment, hardly ever spoke and always avoided looking at him.

"Ah, Mr. Carlton, you've been working too hard," Mr. Ortega said. "You don't look well."

Mrs. Ortega fetched a glass of water and handed it to the afflicted man. He sipped merely to moisten his mouth, then he put the glass down on the table.

"A man has to know when to take it easy," Mr. Ortega philosophized.

"It's the heat. It's been too hot a day for this time of year," Carlton said dejectedly.

"Your color is not good at all," Mrs. Ortega said. "You look green. Yes, green all over your face."

"You need a little shot of something," Mr. Ortega said. "Water won't do at times like these."

"All I need is to catch my breath."

"I have a little rum here in the cupboard for just such an emergency. You never know when a little something is going to come in handy." Mr. Ortega pulled out the bottle and a glass.

"Thank you, but I think I better not," Carlton said.

"Come, you must, for your health."

"I'm not a drinking man."

Mr. Ortega shrugged his shoulder and did not insist.

"You don't look comfortable in that chair," Mrs. Ortega said solicitously.

Indeed, Carlton was too big for the chair. His immense body had swallowed the chair, and he seemed to be supported by only four thin metal tubes. It had occurred to Mrs. Ortega that the chair might not withstand so great a weight and that she would then be out of a chair from the very set that had been purchased from Mr. Carlton. She would feel better if he sat in the living room, where his bulk could be more easily accommodated and where he might notice that the furniture, bought from him also, and not even half paid yet, was not holding up well.

"I'm fine," Carlton said, trying to get on his feet. "I really must get going."

Really, he didn't feel at all confident in his ability to descend the stairs. He didn't know what was happening to him. He would have stumbled as he got up from the chair had not Mr. Ortega supported him and led him into the living room where he was deposited in one of the armchairs. Mrs. Ortega noted that Mr. Carlton's hand rested on the frayed piping of the upholstery and that he could plainly see that the material was of very poor quality. She wondered how he avoided feeling guilty for having supplied inferior goods at what she now considered an exorbitant price.

Nothing could have been further from Georgie Carlton's mind. He was absorbed in his own misfortune. All day he had been depressed. He had gotten up that morning with a lump in his throat and a haze over his eyes. Everything he looked at seemed to be covered by a thin film of soapy water. He had no explanation as to why he felt that way this day in particular. The symptom, common enough, did not arouse any extraordinary conjecture on his part. He accepted the condition as part of the portion allotted to him by fate.

The semidarkness in the room reminded Carlton that the days were growing shorter as winter approached. He hated the winter—the

30

cold, the darkness—Florida was the place for him. The sun would make all the difference. He suddenly remembered that he was sitting in a stranger's living room. Customers were always strangers. "The sun, I like the sun," he said as if in a trance.

"Yes, the sun is a good thing," Mr. Ortega said, puzzled by the sudden utterance.

Mrs. Ortega, mistaking his meaning, walked to the window and lifted the shade as far as it would go, but that didn't appreciably add to the light in the room. "Not much sun this time of day," she said apologetically.

"Not much sun at all," Carlton echoed.

It was Mr. and Mrs. Ortega's turn to be at a loss for what to do next. Mr. Carlton had rarely crossed their threshold before and, on those few occasions, he had but ventured two or three steps beyond it. Now he was in their living room—a quite disconcerting development. Mrs. Ortega's initial anxiety over Mr. Carlton's state of health began to subside. He didn't seem to be getting worse but merely dejected; and that being a familiar state to Mrs. Ortega, she was less inclined to be alarmed. That left her free to entertain the thought that she disliked Mr. Carlton.

Mr. Ortega tried to muster the proper attitude to display when conversing with the well-to-do. "How's business?" he asked. But the look of chagrin on Carlton's face made Mr. Ortega fear that he had overstepped.

"If you only knew," was Carlton's reply. "If you only knew."

That wasn't much help to Mr. Ortega. "Must be good," he said. "Everybody needs what you sell."

When Carlton's eyes seemed about to produce tears, Mrs. Ortega, who had stepped into the kitchen from where she still kept an eye on Carlton, again became alarmed. Seeing Carlton in such a state, she concluded that he was suffering from a serious illness. Such a heavy person was surely unhealthy. She imagined Carlton dropping dead right there in her living room. She saw a certain comic side to

Carlton's lying lifeless on the floor; but being a practical woman, she was immediately assailed by thoughts of the inevitable unpleasantness that would follow. She wished that he would get up and leave. She wished that he had not come at all.

Mr. Ortega ignored Carlton's distress. "Business like yours must rake in the cash," he said. "I wanted to go into business for myself when I was younger," he added, his voice trailing off as if he had involved himself in too complicated a thought. "Yes, I would have done it, had I been able to get a little capital," he added as if talking to himself. The spontaneous lie was born under duress, and he would not remember it the next day.

Noticing Mr. Ortega's discomfort, Carlton concluded that he was imposing on his clients in an unprofessional manner. He was as anxious to leave, but he felt paralyzed. He began to suspect that his ailment was not physical. The possibility that some other agency was keeping him in the Ortegas' apartment brought on a wave of panic that he tried to assuage by being more attentive to his host. "We're none of us as young as we used to be," he said trying to carry some of the conversation, while at the same time excusing and reassuring himself. "Climbing up and down stairs is for the young."

"It's not for a man to work all day and some of the night too," Mr. Ortega said.

Carlton failed to catch the drift. He was thinking of the person who might take the load off his shoulders. "I have a son," he said, "but he won't have anything do with my business. At first, I thought that's all right; maybe he'll do better. Who needs to work sixteen hours a day? He'll go to college, make something of himself. Not that he ever showed himself to be a scholar, but that never stopped anybody from going to college, did it?"

Mr. Ortega nodded noncommittally.

"So I sent him to college out in the Midwest. That's where he wanted to go. And what it cost, you can't imagine. So at the Christmas break, does he come home? He goes to San Francisco, and I know nothing about it. Ships out as a merchant seaman on a boat to Peru. For eight months, I don't hear a word, then he shows up at my door, with a wife yet. Not an ordinary girl, mind you. This one wants to be on the stage, a professional singer, only she has no voice, looks maybe, but no voice. But my son believes in her, and she believes in herself, so she keeps taking lessons and going to auditions. No sense, no sense at all. Nothing I can do."

Overwhelmed by helplessness and panic, the journey that had taken him from the door to the living room puzzled him. He was not supposed to be sitting in that chair, feeling sick when he was collecting a payment. The longer he sat, the worse the situation became. Over this shoulder, he shot a glance at the door. A short distance, he figured it was less than twenty feet from where he sat, but those twenty feet seemed fraught with innumerable dangers. He didn't fear anything from Mr. and Mrs. Ortega. They weren't the threat, but he resented their being safe when he wasn't.

Mrs. Ortega again became alarmed. "Someone should come and get you," she said. "You can't go home alone." She ordered Juan to call the store.

"No, don't bother," Carlton said. "There's nobody there."

"Home then, your son."

"No use," he said, "no use." He got up to go.

Almost at the door, he remembered the reason for being at the Ortegas'. He turned and faced Mrs. Ortega. She was ready for him and handed him the payment booklet with the five dollars in it. He took it, scribbled on it with a pencil, pocketed the money, marked his own record card, and handed the booklet back to Mrs. Ortega. The friendliness had gone out of her eyes.

She held the door open for him, and he propelled himself into the awaiting hallway. She listened to his footsteps descending the stairs.

"That man doesn't have long for this world," she said.

Juan Ortega shrugged his shoulder.

"Maybe you should go down and see that he gets to his car all right."

"No sense going up and down those stairs," he said, and he sat down to read the *Daily News*.

Photographs

SOMETIMES MARIO PRAYED for things to happen. When the bases were loaded, he prayed that he would hit a home run. His prayers usually went unanswered. Raymond Cazzario, on the other hand, said he didn't believe in God, and yet, he was the best stickball player on the block. Perhaps God had more important things to do than watch stickball games.

Mario prayed in school, but it didn't do him any good there either. Praying only kept him from having bad dreams. He prayed at night before going to bed. Very tired one night, he skipped his prayers; the devil roamed through his dreams. He said his prayers every night after that whether he was tired or not; but after a while, it occurred to him that the dreams and the prayers might not have had anything to do with each other, that it had been a coincidence that he had a nightmare the same night that he skipped his prayers.

He recalled the time he shot marbles against Junior Figueroa, the champion marble shooter of Rogers Place, a title Junior held until he moved away and, no doubt, became champion marble shooter on his new block. Anyway, in a match against Junior, Mario was getting cleaned out. Raymond Cazzario slipped Mario a rabbit's foot key chain. "Here's for luck," he said. Mario clutched the rabbit's-foot in his left hand and shot with his right. Whammo! He hit the very next shot. Mario kept gaining until Junior had only three marbles left and he called it quits.

The next day, Junior asked for a rematch. Raymond again, because he didn't like Junior, lent Mario the rabbit's foot. But this time the lucky charm had no effect. Maybe it was the same with prayers. He decided to put the matter to a test, and he again went to bed without praying. He dreamed that the devil was chasing him. He tried to call out for his mother to save him, but no sound came out of his mouth.

He woke up afraid that if he drowsed off he would die. Only after he said his prayers did he fall back to sleep.

His mother, Doña Clementina, prayed all the time. Mario watched her kneeling, rosary in hand, by the side of the bed, her fingers going from bead to bead as her lips moved silently. She turned from the rosary and saw him standing there.

"My children don't understand," she said. "They don't understand. It's my punishment."

"You're always saying that," he said. "Stop saying that."

"We all have to bear our cross," she said.

"What cross? What cross?"

"Please stop shouting," she commanded.

"I'm not shouting!" he retorted. He didn't want to hear about crosses or churches. He went to his room and laid on the bottom part of the bunk bed that took up most of the space. From a half-open closet clothes spilled out. He didn't turn on the light but lay in the semidarkness. He lay there a while, without moving, thinking of his mother in the other room praying.

He took down a photograph album from the top shelf of the closet. At moments like these, looking at the photographs made him feel better. There were many pictures of when he and his brother and sister were younger and still lived in Bayamon. He didn't bother to turn on the light. He had looked at the photographs so often that he didn't need the light. He felt better without it.

There was a picture of him and his mother standing in front of a house. They both squinted, the sun in their eyes, because his father, Don Juan, always took pictures with the sun at his back. "Don't squint. Don't squint," he would always say, but there was no helping it. Doña Clementina was young in the pictures. Mario was constantly surprised at how much his mother had changed.

He remembered that house as if it had been in a dream. The roof leaked when it rained. His mother would put pots on the floor to catch the water. He remembered sticking the muzzle of his cap pistol through cracks between the wall slats to shoot the outlaws who tramped into town on the path that ran by the house.

"What are you doing, Mario?" his mother called from the kitchen.

"I'm shooting the bad guys."

"Come here and bring that gun."

She took the pistol, held it by the muzzle, and stooped by the stove. In her other hand, she held a broom and stuck it under the stove. As she raised the gun over her head, a rat darted from the dark space. The butt of the gun came down missing the rodent but making a loud noise on hitting the floor. Mario put his hands over his ears. Doña Clementina swung at the rat again before it disappeared through a hole in the floor.

"Let me do it next time!" Mario shouted.

"Sure, why not?" she said. She handed the toy gun back to him.

Doña Clementina had been a beautiful woman when she was young. Everyone said so, and the photographs proved it. When Mario remembered her chasing the rat, he remembered her as she was in the pictures.

In another photograph, Mario stood in the garden of the hospital where his father worked. The boy in the image was very thin, and his hair stuck out at the crown, straight in all directions. The doctor lived across the road in a two-story concrete house painted white, a stone eagle on the roof. People talked a great deal about the eagle when it was first put up. No one had ever seen a stone eagle on the roof of a house. Mario's father and Fernando, the doctor's son, were buddies. Mario remembered driving in a car with his father and Fernando. They stopped at a house on the outskirts of town. "Stay here," his father said. "I'll be back in a few minutes." The two men went into the house. From the car, Mario heard music and laughing and women's voices in the house. In a while his father returned. "Come, let's take you home," he said. He smelled of rum.

2

On his way home from the hospital, Mario cut across the pasture, careful not to step in one of the many coils of cow dung scattered over the field. The cows belonged to the hospital. Everyday at five o'clock Paco herded them to a shed near the doctor's house. Mario followed to watch Paco milk the cows.

A big man with large hands, Paco sat on a stool and began milking. Rhythmically, the streams of milk hit the bottom of the tin pail—milk, milk / milk, milk / milk, milk. The cow, trying to swat flies with its tail, smacked Paco. One, two, three times Paco was smacked before he remembered to tie the cow's tail to her legs. Every day he was smacked before he remembered.

Sometimes Mario wondered whether he was any smarter than Paco. He looked across the road that divided the pasture. A guava tree stood in the middle of the field. He had been stupid to climb that tree without noticing the beehive and the guavas not ripe yet. He shivered remembering the bee stings. Beyond the guava tree a bamboo grove swayed, and beyond that flowed a stream. Behind the bamboo grove, by the stream, the hospital dumped garbage. Mario showed his mother a syringe he had found by the stream. It was terrible to see her angry. He didn't walk by the stream anymore after that.

3

His mother's hair fell over her shoulders down to her waist. They went out through the back door of the house. The chickens scurried out of the way as they crossed the yard. They followed the path through the woods. He watched his mother as she walked in front of him. He ran up to look at her face. It was a good face except when it was angry. She stood on one foot and bent to remove one sandal then the other. She attached them to the belt of her dress. As they walked on, the earth clung to her feet.

"Can I take my shoes off too?"

"No," she said, "we're almost there."

When they reached the barbed wire, they crawled under it. Mario knew exactly what to do. They picked tomatoes and hot peppers. Mario put the peppers in his pockets and the tomatoes in his shirt.

Suddenly, his mother crouched and pulled him down. They listened to the rustling of leaves. They moved along the ground toward the wire, Mario ahead of his mother. He turned to look. She was trying not to giggle. They crawled under the wire the same way they had come. Then they stood up, so that the man would see them. He shouted at them, but he would not crawl under the wire. When they were out of reach, they stopped to laugh.

4

Mario had locked the door of the room so that he might continue looking at the pictures in peace. He heard Pedrito's footsteps.

Pedrito banged on the door. "Hey, let me in!" he shouted. He was loud like his mother.

"Go away," Mario said. "Leave me alone."

"If you don't open up, I'm going to knock the door down. It's my room too, ya know!"

"Stop shouting," Mario said fearing that his mother would soon intervene.

Pedrito rammed his shoulder against the door.

Doña Clementina came out of her room. "*Que hacen? Ah? Que hacen?* You want to knock the house down? You want to kill me! That's what you want. I know that's what you want!"

"Mario won't let me in," Pedrito screamed at her.

"If you bang that door again, I'm going to break every bone in your body," she shouted.

Again, Pedrito ran into the door.

"*Bruto! Animal!* Don't you have any respect?" She sobbed as tears ran down her cheeks. "I'll teach you!"

"Open that door," Pedrito kept shouting and beating on it with his fist.

Mario flung the door open to see his mother in a frenzy beating Pedrito. In one hand she still held the rosary. Pedrito ran through the open door, slammed and bolted it.

Doña Clementina now banged on the door. "*Sin vergüenzas!* Is this the way to treat your mother? You're going to drive me to the grave. That's what you're going to do; then you'll be sorry!"

Doña Clementina went back to her room. Mario sat on the bed pretending to be absorbed by the photographs. He heard his sister crying quietly in the living room by herself. She cried whenever there was trouble. Doña Clementina kept shouting about her own misery. Pedrito sat sulking on the bed. Mario regretted not having opened the door right away, but there was nothing he could do now.

"You want to look at the pictures?"

"I don't want to look at no pictures. Don't talk to me."

"Here's one of you throwing dirt in my ear."

"I'm going to beat you up! Boy, am I going to beat you up! If you say another word, I'm going kick your balls," Pedrito said.

"Look at you when you was a baby. You was a cute baby," Mario said, his head down as if looking at the photo but watching his brother out of the corner of his eye. Perhaps Pedrito would cool off, but just in case, Mario braced himself for a fierce onslaught. Pedrito was stubborn. He would fight even when there was no possibility of winning. Sometimes, when Don Juan beat him with a strap, he held back the tears and refused to cry.

Pedrito gazed at the picture of himself as a baby throwing dirt at his brother's ear. He relaxed. He didn't want to fight with his brother. They fought a great deal, but that didn't mean anything. They had to look after each other. Pedrito moved to the edge of the bed and rested his back against the wall. In the semidarkness, they kept looking through the album. There were pictures of each of them standing in the snow all alone, their coats identical.

"Do you remember how it was before we came to the Bronx?" Pedrito asked.

"Yeah, some. It was nice."

"Why did we come here?"

"I guess so Papi could get a better job. Or maybe it was because..."

"Because what?"

"The nurse."

"What nurse?"

"Papi worked at a hospital. He got a love letter from this nurse, and Mami found it in his pocket."

"I didn't know that," Pedrito said, his face veiled by the darkness.

"I don't know it either, really. It was long ago. Nobody talks about it anymore."

They sat in silence for a long time.

A Higher Education

Finley Hall

STEPHEN AND I hung out in the Finley Hall cafeteria. A steady stream of students moved up and down the aisles—the noise a constant din. Several of my classmates from the poetry writing class often joined us there, Laura one of them. The first time she met Stephen, she immediately became intimate.

"Oh, I wish I knew what to do," she said as she sat down. "This guy keeps writing me love letters. I don't know what to do." A grimace distorted her wide mouth. Surrounded by red tresses, the oily pale skin of her freckled face looked translucent.

"That's a problem?" Stephen asked.

Laura stared at him, examining his look—the bushy eyebrows and blue eyes that gave the lie to the sneer constantly on his lips. She later admitted that she thought him handsome and commanding. She drew herself up and pursed her lips like a child aware of her ability to create a disturbance. "I'm married," she declared.

"You're a married lady?" Stephen exclaimed. "You don't look married."

"What's that supposed to mean?"

"You look so young," he said.

"Laura is not like the rest of us," I attempted to clarify. "She's a graduate student."

"You keep very well," Stephen mirthfully said and looked over at me to see if I concurred that she was indeed an oddity. "So you like to hang out with us younger folk."

"We're in the special writing class together," I tried to explain our acquaintance.

"The one you can enroll by invitation only?"

"That's the one," Laura said with a smirk, but she quickly changed the subject and resumed alluding to her personal problem. "I

45

shouldn't be telling you all this," she said to Stephen. "I hardly know you. Mario is my friend, but you're a complete stranger."

"Nah, I'm your friend too. Friendship doesn't depend on time. Some people are the best of friends from the minute they meet. I can help you. I have lots of experience with problems of the heart."

"You have?"

"Yeah, ask Mario. He'll tell you."

"Well, I have to talk. You know, that's one of my problems. I can't keep from talking. I like you, you know, as a friend I mean. You seem so sincere."

"Yes, I'm very sincere. Sincerity is one of the most important qualities in a person."

"And you don't know Jay, that's my husband," she continued. "So it doesn't matter what I say."

"Even if I knew him, it wouldn't matter."

"I don't know what to do about Sam," she said.

"Sam Bauer you're talking about?" I asked surprised.

"He's a little crazy. Don't get me wrong, I wouldn't want to get seriously involved with him, but I do think he's brilliant."

"Yes, he is," I said.

"You mean he's brilliant in bed?" Stephen asked.

"I mean he's a brilliant intellect," Laura answered having taken the question seriously.

"I don't see why that should be a consideration," Stephen said. "After all, what you want is a good lay."

Jumping up, she exclaimed, "What a crude way of talking!" She seemed about to burst into tears.

Stephen held her hand. "Don't be upset," he said. "I'm sorry. I didn't mean to offend. I'm sorry. I really am."

Still looking distraught, she sat down again.

"You want to have a fling with him?"

"That's what I don't know."

"You should," Stephen emphatically said. "In matters of the

heart, when in doubt, act. That's my motto. Unless, of course, you're madly in love with your husband."

"I am," she said.

"Then why Sam?" I asked, adding a tone of censure to the conversation.

"A very interesting point," Stephen said.

"He hasn't. . . we haven't. . . I don't know how to say this. You see, he hasn't. . . touched me. You know what I mean? In months."

"That's terrible!" Stephen exclaimed. "That's uncivilized."

"You really think so?"

"I wouldn't say so if I didn't."

"There's Rick," I said, looking over to the aisle. "Hey Rick! Over here!" I called.

A corpulent young man with very dark hair and circles under his eyes sauntered over, his gait semigraceful if somewhat comic, his face distorted by a grin.

"You wouldn't believe what a mind-blowing experience I just had," he said in a voice artificially deep. He was a constant smoker. "This school thing can really sock it to you sometimes. I just can't believe that last hour. I mean it's the kind of thing that happens, what, maybe once a year? What am I talking about? It might happen once in four years. It might never happen. I am telling you, it was really something."

"You haven't told us anything yet," Stephen said.

"I haven't told you anything, and I've told you everything. Can you dig that? If you dig it, then you got it. If you don't dig it, then there's no sense in my explaining it. You see that's the beauty of this kind of thing. It's not susceptible to words. Words bounce off of it, slide off, like water off a duck's back."

"I know what you mean about words," I said, having finally acquired the knack of talking to Rick.

"I knew you would," Rick said. "I knew you would, I mean, I know you're beautiful. You see the potential. Yeah, potential, that's it. That's it, isn't it? The potential in the moment is what has to be grasped. I mean it's like the juice in an orange, right? Yeah, that's what it's like. Jesus, that's beautiful! I can't believe I said that, juice in the orange. You have to squeeze it. All your life you have to squeeze every moment."

"Yes," Laura said, "I know what you mean."

"I don't. What happened in the class?" Stephen asked. "I hear much art and no matter."

"What happened was rapport, man, you know what that means? Can you dig oneness? Well, can you?"

"I *dig* it," Stephen answered, his eyebrows rising on the word "dig."

"Well, that's it, man. You got it. That's what happened, oneness with your fellow men, with nature, with God. That's what happened. That's all."

"I have to break the rapport with you people right now," Laura said, "because I have a class." She got up to go. "See you later Mario and you too Rick. And I certainly hope to see you again soon," she said to Stephen. She headed for the exit, and we watched her slightly bowed legs move her drooping body toward the door.

When she was out of sight Stephen asked, "Where did you dig her up? She looks like a Raggedy Ann, and she could use new stuffing."

"How can you sit there and make fun of her behind her back?" Rick let loose. "I mean, I don't dig you at all. You sit down with somebody, and the minute her back's turned you're down on her. I mean, what is it with you? Jesus Christ, you are something else. Laura there, she's got problems. She doesn't need you making fun of her."

"What's the difference? She didn't hear what I said, so she's none the worse."

"Oh man, you're too much. I don't believe you're for real."

"Well, listen Rick, I would love to argue with you," Stephen said, "but I have work to do. I'm going over to Cohen and do some reading."

"Maybe we can go for a beer later on," I said.

"I'll call you tonight," Stephen said.

"Okay."

"Take it easy, Rick," Stephen said and sauntered off to the library.

"Don't be upset, Rick," I said. "He didn't mean anything. He talks like that, but he wouldn't hurt anybody."

"You don't see," Rick said. "You don't see because you're his friend."

"True," I said. "He is my friend, and I do need friends."

"What you need is a woman to be serious about, Mario. A man is nothing without a woman."

"I just haven't found the right one. What can I say? I'm unlucky with women."

"It's not luck, man; it's not luck. Look around, just in this room there are so many women. There's got to be one for you right here."

I glanced around and spied Gail Wasserman sitting a few tables away. I considered the shape of her face perfect. I didn't know why it had such an effect on me. After all, many beautiful women didn't have faces shaped that way. Gail's face was unique. I imagined running my fingers through her long black hair that fell to the middle of her back. Her large eyes accentuated with eyeliner achieved a crisp appearance. Ordinarily, I would have found that look harsh; but on Gail, the roundness of her face overcame the severity of the makeup. She verged on extraordinarily attractive plumpness. However, she had no interest in me and always acted haughty and cold.

"She's the kind of woman I go for," I said to Rick.

Rick turned to look in Gail's direction. "The one with the dark hair?" he asked.

"Yeah."

Rick made a face of disapproval. "That's not what you want," he said. "She's a cold fish. She's probably frigid."

"You can tell just by looking at her?"

"Yeah, I can tell."

"Rick, you're crazy, and even if she were, she would thaw eventually."

"Maybe, but why wait?"

"I can't explain why, Rick," I said, and we left it at that.

That evening, Stephen drove his Beetle down from Pelham Manor to Rogers Place to pick me up. We headed for the Riviera, his favorite bar in Greenwich Village. We sat at a table with a view of the avenue, and the waiter came over.

"Steamed clams and two drafts," Stephen said.

The young man in a white shirt and black trousers, order pad in hand, gingerly said, "I have to ask you guys for ID. I'm really sorry, but they make me do that, you understand."

"No problem," Stephen said.

We pulled out our wallets where our draft cards rested behind our student IDs. We each pulled out the draft card and offered it to the waiter.

"All right," he said. Without examining them, he retreated to fill the order.

"You like steamed clams, don't you?" Stephen asked me.

"I've never had any."

"Well, just try them," he said with an insouciant smile on his face. He was out to have fun educating me.

The waiter brought the clams and the beer and placed them on the table. "Enjoy," he said. He had yet to recover from having asked for ID.

"Go ahead, have some clams," Stephen urged. I tasted but wasn't impressed. I stuck with the beer and the pretzels. After two beers, Stephen suggested we pay a visit to a friend of his on West Street. He got up and walked over to the pay phone. He made a call and then came back to the table. "She's interesting," he said as if attempting to convince me to follow him on the excursion. He called for the check, and the waiter brought it over. "Tonight is on me," Stephen said. He left a big tip, twice as much as customary. "He's a nice guy," he said as if he had to explain his generosity.

We drove a few blocks to West Street. Approaching the piers, the neighborhood structures became warehouses, the street darker without the lights of the bars, restaurants, and clubs the farther we moved from Sheridan Square. The west side of the Village, caught in a time warp, seemed a century behind the rest of the city, the streets still paved with cobblestones and the street lamps reminiscent of the days of gaslights.

"The easy parking at night is the good thing, no shortage of spots," Stephen said pulling up to the curb on West Street. "Hard to believe she lives here."

"Tell me again; who's this person we're visiting?"

"She's a fellow classmate of ours," Stephen said in a droll tone.

We ascended the steps of the four-story brick building. When we got to the third floor, Stephen knocked on the door, but there was no answer. The door opened when he turned the knob. "I suppose everyone's welcome," he said. The door led into a kitchen where the minimal lighting in the room cast a blue shade on everything. Glancing at the sink full of dirty dishes, I imagined that in the daylight everything looked worse, something to be said in favor of darkness.

At the other end of the kitchen a bead curtain hung over the opening. Stephen called out, "Leila!" We waited for an answer but none came. After calling out her name again, a mumbled response emerged from the darkness.

"I think she said come in, right?" Stephen queried turning his head in my direction.

Not having recognized a single word, I shrugged my shoulder. Stephen parted the bead curtain, and I followed him to the next room, where a candle flickered on a night table by the bed. Leila's back rested on the pillow against the headboard. A sleeping figure stretched beside her. Leila, less than alert and her companion already asleep, raised a joint to her lips and took a drag. Recognizing her, I had a sensation reminiscent of a fragile object falling to the floor and splintering into innumerable pieces.

I had never spoken to Leila, but I had observed her as she dashed across the campus from one class to another. When I had first noticed her, her look had struck me, her eyes an unusual color that went along with facial features just as distinctive. In plain daylight, the uniqueness of her look had triggered my imagination, but seeing her at the moment in the bed, stoned, another derelict by her side, the glamour of her campus image vanished.

She extended her hand offering Stephen the joint. He declined.

"I guess you're not in the mood for company," he said.

She didn't answer but just took another drag.

"Well, see you back in class," he said.

She nodded her head.

We descended out to the street where Stephen's containment broke down. "She's just a slut," he said.

Silently, we got back into the car.

The next day, exiting Finley and heading north, I strolled leisurely contemplating the changing leaves of the oaks and maples that adorned the grounds leading to the Morris Cohen Library. I spied Isabel walking down from the North Campus. I waved to her and she waved back. She wore tight jeans and boots that reached halfway up her calves. I once suggested to her that maybe we were meant for each other, and she laughed and said, "Definitely not."

The weather still warm, many students sat outside on the library steps and on the stone fence separating the tennis courts from the walkway. Tennis directly in front of the library made an odd combination. I never saw anyone play on those courts. I walked up the library steps to look for an article assigned in a course on the philosophy of language, "Is Truth a Necessary Condition for Knowledge?" The title had a nice ring to it. Intrigued by the question, I wondered about the possible answers.

Karen

*B*EFORE GOING HOME *for the evening, my eyes search the Great Lawn for a glimpse of Sharon. Love, is it? Yes, I love her passionately though I know nothing about her. Title for a scholarly paper: "Is Knowledge a Necessary Condition for Love?" With ironclad logic a distinguished researcher demonstrates that knowledge of the life, character, and antecedents of the subject are superfluous to one who has contracted the ailment of falling in love—a subject worthy of further study.*

I know next to nothing about Sharon. Merely her image captivates me—eyes outlined in black, her full-lipped face sensual, perhaps her mouth a little too wide. When she crosses her legs, the flesh of her thighs folds into itself, too much flesh perhaps. She verges on being too much yet not quite enough. Her manner virginal, she is refined, always impeccably dressed. She has different guises that create uncertainty. A chameleon really, now she has short brown hair, her eyes still blue, her skin not as milky soft. Did she age? Perhaps. Age shows around her neck; the flesh along the jawbone sags. She does not age prettily, but what does that matter?

She condescends to be distantly friendly. She has a boyfriend stashed away somewhere. "In Canada," she says, "to avoid the draft." I take heart, my rival far away. Perhaps Sharon will forget him; perhaps he won't come back. When she isn't near, anxiety overwhelms me; every moment away from her is preparation to be with her.

Riding the subway every morning, I look forward to seeing her, the mere sight of her a salve. In the evenings, I ride away, another day gone by and I have again failed to win her over. All the way home, I think of her and look forward to the next day. I know her schedule by heart. I roam the halls of the student center looking for her. My pain will cease as soon as I see her. I will have a moment of overwhelming joy as she turns her head to notice me, her voluptuous lips parting in an involuntary smile. Hardly will I have begun to speak to her when my anxiety returns as I realize that time is quickly passing. Momentarily, she will have to leave en route to her next class. At night, I dream of her running through a blue landscape. When she reaches the horizon, the moon swallows her.

Forlorn, gazing across the Great Lawn, I stood in front of Finley Hall. The yellowing leaves on the trees announced the inevitable change of season. As I contemplated nature's preparation for the harshness to come, I sensed someone by my side. I turned to see a face wanting to speak to me.

"We're in the same Latin class," she said.

In her baggy blue jeans, her hair braided, Karen had a disarming look. In class, I had noticed that she never wore makeup, her Irish face a beacon of health. Exactly what an old world peasant woman in full bloom would look like, I thought, never having seen the old world nor its peasants. Her two rather large front teeth failed to detract from her charm. Talking about life in general, we stood at the entrance of Finley Hall for a while then strolled to the North Campus and back in earnest conversation. "Walk me home," she said. We ambled down Convent Avenue and across 127th Street to the housing projects. At the door of the building, I began to say good-bye.

"Come up," she said.

"I wouldn't want to intrude on your family."

"If you don't want to come up, say so," she admonished, "but don't make that excuse."

We rode the elevator to the fourteenth floor. Her mother, a large, gray-haired woman with gaps between her teeth, perfunctorily greeted us as we entered the apartment. I wondered whether she had noticed me at all. Past the kitchen, in the living room, Karen's younger sister and brother stared at the television as they ate sitting on a couch torn in several places. A couple of fruit crates served as tables. No one took any interest in me.

"We can eat in my room," Karen said.

The strangeness transformed the sordidness of the place. For all I knew, or wanted to know, she was a swan, a firebird, a princess in disguise. Her barely furnished room contained a bed, a dresser, and a bicycle propped up against the wall.

"Sit down," she said. "I'll get us some food."

She brought back rice and fried fish, and we ate sitting on her bed.

"You read lots of books, don't you?" she said.

"Yea, I suppose you could say that," I guardedly responded having surmised her distrust of books.

On our walk, we had discussed her dissatisfaction with being at the college. She was going to drop out soon, she said. She didn't see much point in a college education—all books.

"Real life is better," she said. "You learn more from real life."

"Books are like people," I retorted. "You can learn from them or not. It's up to you."

A touch of condescension emanated from her look, a bemusement at the enormity of the task of trying to save me from so great an error. I countered with a semblance of superiority of my own; I would humor her, benignly gloss over her ignorance.

"I have a favorite book," she said. "*The Little Prince*, have you read it?"

I hadn't.

"It's a great book," she said. "You must read it."

"I will," I said.

"No, really, you must promise."

"I promise," I said. I figured I could get it at the campus bookstore. "I'll get a copy on Monday."

"I'll lend you my copy," she said springing up and going to the closet. She pulled the book from the top shelf. "We can read it now."

I looked through the first few pages.

"We can take turns reading," she said. "You read first."

I started to read out loud. I was shocked. Even about books she had something to teach me. Taking turns until we tired, we read about fifty pages.

"You can take it and finish it at home," she said.

Already late, I gathered myself to leave.

"You don't have to go," she said. "You can stay with me tonight."

She misread the look on my face and took my silence as a possible refusal. "You can sleep in the living room or in my brother's room," she said, and after a pause she added, "or here with me."

Again I hesitated. "What about your parents?" I managed to ask.

"My mother is so drunk she doesn't even know you're here. Didn't you notice her eyes were glazed?"

I shook my head. I hadn't bothered to interpret her mother's look.

"My father works nights," she continued. "You can leave tomorrow morning before anybody else gets up.

"You don't have to sleep with me," she repeated. "Are you staying?"

"All right," I said.

"Where do you want to sleep?"

As I recovered my wits, her game of choice annoyed me.

"I'm staying with you," I said.

She fetched me a towel and showed me the way to the bathroom. "You can use my toothbrush if you want to," she said.

"No, I'll just rinse," I said.

When I got back to her bedroom, she was undressing. "I sleep with the windows open," she said. "It's healthier that way, get some fresh air. You don't mind, do you?"

"It's all right," I said. My knees shook as I climbed out of my dungarees. "I don't have a condom," I said.

"Doesn't matter," she responded nonchalantly. "We don't have to do it that way."

She turned off the light. My hair bristled, my skin electrified then passed into quietness. Her legs twined around me. I could hear a hum from inside of her, her body singing. Yet, I hesitated, not knowing what she expected of me exactly. Was there a proper procedure, a protocol? I didn't know.

In the middle of the night a noise woke me. I became instantly alert.

"What's the matter?" she whispered, stirring next to me.

"That noise?"

"It's my father home from work," she said. "He's drunk."

I marveled at the ease of her delivery. A totally different world from the one I was used to, and she, certainly different from any other woman I knew, never equivocated. I held her closely and fell asleep.

We were up early and out of the house before anyone else got up. On that cool and misty morning, she walked me to St. Nicholas Terrace.

"I'll see you on Monday," I said, inhaling her fragrance as I kissed her.

"I'll see you," she said and turned to walk back through the campus.

As I descended the park steps, I surveyed the familiar landscape. Like a bird fluttering out of the brush and instantly disappearing into nearby foliage, Sharon's image flitted before me. Content at the moment, I ignored it.

Lucile

THE SUMMER BEFORE my senior year, I got a job as a counselor at a day camp operated from the public housing near Tremont Avenue. Just a few blocks away, I still lived with my parents, a situation I was anxious to change. My Regent Scholarship insufficient for housing, I looked forward to a paycheck that, along with a student loan, would allow me to rent an apartment.

At the day camp, along with two junior counselors, teen-age girls, to help me, I took a group of ten-year-olds to activities in nearby parks, swimming at the public pool, once a week a bus excursion to a more distant place, a beach or an amusement park. The job manageable but exhausting, two of the children hyperactive and needing to be closely watched added to the travail. Always glad to be back at the center, I sat down at the end of the day. Often, Lucile Hathaway, the younger of the junior counselors, pulled up a chair and sat close to me.

"You know why my skin is so light?" she asked me.

Only one answer I could think of as I looked at her tan skin, but uncertain as to the propriety of discussing the subject, I kept quiet.

"My father is Italian," she continued.

"Is Hathaway an Italian name?" I asked facetiously, though I wasn't really interested in contradicting her.

"Oh, no, that's my mother's name," Lucile said. "They weren't married. I never met my father."

"I see."

"Do you?"

"Sure," I said though I really didn't know what she wanted me to see.

A few days later, on a trip to Orchard Beach, while the children ate lunch, I laid down on a blanket and having closed my eyes for a second, I felt a hand gently fold into mine. I turned to discover Lucile

58

lying next to me intently gazing into my face and, uncertain of what my response would be, braced for anything.

"You have a nice hand, Lucile, but there's no hand holding on the job."

She released my hand, glad that at least I had waited for her to do so without pushing her away or pulling my hand from hers. At the end of the day, back at the center, she sat in the chair next to mine. "I know that you love me," she said.

"You're a lovely girl, Lucile, but you're too young for me."

"I'm going to be seventeen soon," she said.

"In a couple of years," I said, "you can call me then."

"I'll be seventeen by the end of the summer," she insisted.

"I read your job application, Lucile. I saw your birth date."

"I lied on the application," she said. "I'm legal."

"Legal for what?"

"For whatever you want."

"What I want is for you to go home now, and when you come in tomorrow, we'll smile at each other, and that's it."

"What's the matter? You don't like Italians?"

"I like you fine, Lucile—as a coworker, okay?"

"Okay," she said, "I'll see you tomorrow."

After Lucile left, Janice, the center secretary, came by. Middle-aged, hair straightened, heavy-set woman, in contrast to everyone else in the place she dressed up for work every day as if she were going to a Wall Street office instead of one in a housing project. She stood in front of me and said, "Diane Shapiro needs someone to translate for her. You think you can help her out for a few minutes? She'd really appreciate it."

"Sure," I said. A few more minutes at work to assist the social worker next door made no difference to me. I followed Janice down the hall to the office where a plain-faced young woman sat at her desk.

"Mario here has volunteered to help you, Miss Shapiro," Janice said to the caseworker.

She looked up from the paperwork. "Oh, thank you," she said. Her head twitched slightly. "I have a client who doesn't speak English." Her head twitched again to the right.

I repressed my automatic impulse to imitate her. My body was unconsciously responding to the quirk without any intention of satirizing her malady. I had to watch out.

"I hope you can handle it," she continued. "It's a sad story, cancer and less than a year to live. She's been worried about what will happen to her one child who's mentally deficient and has no guardian. Can you handle all this?"

"Sure," I said, "no problem." As far as I was concerned, translating was an activity that required no emotional involvement.

"I'll be ready in a minute," she said.

Her head twitched several times as she gathered the papers she needed and placed them in her briefcase. She emerged from behind the desk, and I followed her down the hall. Her well-proportioned body made up for her ordinary face. A short walk to the sick woman's door, all the way there Diane talked about the woman's problems. Just to be polite, I pretended to be interested.

No sign of illness was obvious in the woman as she quietly sat in her small, plainly furnished living room. Above the couch hung a large mirror depicting on one side a tiger prowling on a tree branch over a body of water. I recalled a similar mirror that hung in my mother's living room years before until we were evicted, my father having neglected to pay the rent.

"Tell her that I have arranged for her son to be taken care of when the time comes."

I translated everything back and forth. The woman relaxed as if she had nothing else to worry about but her son, and now she was ready for whatever came.

On the way back to the center, Diane said, "You helped me out a great deal. Thank you. How can I repay you?"

"You don't owe me anything."

"Let me take you out to dinner," she said, "as a thank-you. It was hard enough for me to handle this one, and without you, it would have been altogether impossible. I'd feel better if you let me do something for you."

"Let's leave it open," I said. "I'll ask for your advice if I need any on the job. I'm new at working with children."

"Okay," she said, "do come and see me." Her twitching, interrupted during the house call, then resumed.

The following week, on a camp trip to an amusement park, in the haunted house ride, Lucile managed to sit next to me in the last car, from which I had intended to keep an eye on the children riding in the cars ahead of mine. My plan futile, the lighting focused on the exhibits, I could hardly see into the other cars. Lucile, taking advantage, rested her head on my shoulder. In the darkness, I failed to push her away, but on disembarking I rued the fact that I had let her stay, knowing that now she would be more convinced than ever that I welcomed her advances.

After the ride I took her aside and said, "Lucile, you have to stop this."

"Nobody saw us," she said.

"That doesn't matter. You're supposed to be keeping an eye on the children, not chasing after me."

"We can get together on weekends," she said. "I go by your house all the time."

"You know where I live?"

"I followed you home one day. You didn't see me, did you?"

Once, from the stairway window, I had caught a glimpse of someone who resembled Lucile, but by the time I reached the street, the person had disappeared. Concluding that I had been mistaken, I forgot about the incident.

"Lucile, this has to stop," I repeated, but she only walked away grinning.

After dismissing the children that day, I walked by Diane Shapiro's office. She looked up from her papers and beckoned me to come in.

"You look worn out," she said.

I sat down and told her about Lucile.

"Just introduce her to your real girlfriend, and she'll find someone else to fall in love with," Diane's head twitched twice as she spoke.

"That would be simple enough," I said, "if I were involved with someone."

"Just get one of your friends to pretend," she suggested.

"That's a good idea," I continued, "but I don't think any of them is going to want to come up here to put on the act."

"I'll do it," she said. "If you want me to."

"Really?"

"Sure."

"Then I'll owe you."

"No, I'll still take you out to dinner for having helped me with my client."

Next day, at dismissal time, Diane came by. She stood close to me and held my arm just long enough for Lucile to notice. The young woman stared at us as if she had inadvertently stumbled upon her parents in bed together. Disoriented, she walked away to reconsider her approach to the romantic life. Diane, seeing that she had won the first skirmish, decided to press on.

"Why don't we get together on Saturday?" she said as I walked her to the subway. "Then we won't have to pretend anything."

"Sure," I said, meaning that I could think of no objection to seeing her after having searched for one.

That Saturday, I saw her for the first time informally dressed in a white cotton blouse and dungarees. She introduced me to her roommate, Carol, a young woman just out of college. Originally from Pennsylvania, she had come to work in New York. An overfed child, always in fear of not being loved, a trace of petulance on her face tinged her innocent sadness. She straightened out the kitchen before departing for the day.

"I didn't arrange that," Diane informed me once Carol had left. "She was going to be out whether or not you were here."

I let life take its course without any urging or resistance. When

Diane sat next to me on the couch, the placing of my arm over her shoulder was beyond a conscious decision, the events of the moment dictated by her will and desire in the absence of mine. We rolled to the floor soon enough, I aware only of her body and the reaction of mine to its proximity. Only the manifestation of physical conditions to be considered and evaluated, for a moment, I lost control of the action. Suddenly, I became aware of the carpet. As if waking from a trance, the unfamiliarity of the place subdued me, and I rolled away from her. "Weren't we planning to go out?" I asked.

She kept silent for a minute, a silence which she would later point out to me but which at the moment, I failed to notice. "Yes," she said, "that was our plan, but we don't have to keep to it." She sat up and raised her knees holding them with both arms and resting her chin on them. "We're the only ones here for the day, and when night comes, I have my own room anyway."

"Carol doesn't mind if I spend the night?"

"She will if it happens too often, but you can stay tonight."

I did, but the following Saturday I was ready to look for a place of my own. Diane had urged me all week to start my search, so when I went to see her on Saturday, I picked up the *Village Voice* on the way.

"That paper comes out on Wednesdays," she said when I arrived with the folded newspaper in hand. "Everything listed in there is probably gone by now," she continued, piqued by my seeming lack of drive.

"No sense in having a negative attitude," I said. I sat at the kitchen table and, as I opened up the paper, Carol emerged from her room in her nightgown. "You look chipper this morning," I said to her.

She made a face, had a drink of water and went back to her room.

"She's friendly this morning," I buoyantly said.

"She drank too much at a party last night, and she failed to meet a prince."

"Well, that's life," I said as I examined the listings. "Ah, here's something interesting at just the right price."

"It's probably gone."

"Well, let's find out," I said walking over to the phone.

The place still available, I wrote down the address and was ready to go.

"If nobody's taken it yet, it's probably a dump," Diane said.

"How about a quickie to get you out of your negative mood?"

"No, we better go see the apartment."

"It's between Spring and Canal, a block over from Hudson. We'll see the Hard Heart right on the corner of Hudson."

"The what?"

"The Hard Heart," I said shrugging my shoulder. "He said it's a jazz club. It bring crowds to the place on Saturday nights."

"Never heard of it," Diane said.

"I guess you're not into jazz," I said.

We took the subway down to Spring Street and walked west to Renwick Street. On the corner of Hudson we saw the club, the Half Note.

"I thought you said it was the Hard Heart."

"That's what I thought he said."

"I see where your mind is."

"I don't keep secrets from you," I said.

Renwick Street extended for only one block and had only two apartment buildings, one at each end, everything else warehouses, factories, and parking lots for the trucks.

"This is a very out-of-the-way place," Diane said.

"It's not a slum," I said, prone to look at the positive side when in her company. I wondered how long that would last.

D'Anuncio, the agent, was a middle-aged man whose hands quivered, the malady especially noticeable when he maneuvered a cigarette. I kept wondering whether the tip of the cigarette would miss his lips. I nervously watched expecting the scene to be pitiful, but D'Anuncio managed his disability much more adroitly than I anticipated. After observing the cigarette rise successfully to his lips a few times, I got used to it, just as I had grown accustomed to Diane's twitch.

The apartment, on the second floor, had only two rooms, one of them a kitchen with a bathtub compartment next to the sink.

"Where's the bathroom?" Diane asked.

"Out in the hall," D'Anuncio said.

"It has to be shared?" A wave of panic undulated over her face.

"Oh, no," said D'Anuncio. "It's your own bathroom with a lock." He pointed to a key that hung from a nail by the door.

"Still, it's not as good as having the bathroom inside," she said.

"No, it's not, but only the apartments on the other side of the building have the bathrooms inside."

Although not too happy about the bathroom being in the hall, I figured I would get used to it. Diane didn't make too much of a fuss about it. "I kind'a like it," I said. "And it's just what I can afford."

"It's nice enough," Diane agreed. "You want it?"

"I think so," I said.

"For fifty dollars you can have the furniture," D'Anuncio said taking the cigarette out of his mouth, his hand quivering. He was talking about a table, chairs, a dresser, and a bed. "Otherwise I'll have it moved out," he continued.

"It's your furniture?" Diane asked.

"The previous tenant left it behind when he disappeared without paying the last month's rent."

"He just vanished?"

"He must've been running away from something," D'Anuncio said, his face implying that he knew more than he was telling.

"I'll take it," I said.

"So you're taking the apartment too?" D'Anuncio asked, humor behind his straight face.

"What's on the other side of that door?" Diane inquired pointing to another door in the kitchen.

"That door stays locked," D'Anuncio said. "It's just a closet used for storing the maintenance equipment. There's another door to it from the hallway. Occasionally the cleaning man goes in there to get the mop and pail and things like that."

"All right," I said.

Downstairs, in D'Anuncio's place, I signed the lease and gave him a month's rent plus a month's security and the fifty dollars for the furniture. Having received the key to the apartment, Diane and I went back up to reinspect. Opening the top drawer of the dresser, I found three photos obviously shot in the apartment. A nude woman, shyly smiling, revealed her discomfort about being photographed.

"The former tenant had a girlfriend," I said.

"To leave those pictures he must've been in a hurry when he moved," Diane commented looking over my shoulder.

"Maybe he left them as souvenirs."

"Do you suppose she left pictures of him?"

"They're probably in the bottom drawer."

"I don't think so," she said opening the drawer.

"I'll have to take pictures of you to leave when I move," I said. I laid down on the bed.

"Don't get on that bed," Diane exclaimed. "It may have bugs!"

"I don't see any. Come, let's initiate it."

"I'm not getting on that bed without spraying it, and we need sheets."

"Oh, come on, we didn't have sheets on your floor."

"I know who sleeps on my floor, but I don't know who's been on that bed."

"You can be on top. You don't have to touch the bed."

"Oh, yeah?"

"Sure," I said pulling her over.

At the day camp, I still had a difficult time with Lucile. Unwilling to give up, whenever Diane came by at the end of the day, Lucile kept an eye on us. I had expected her to drop me and run after someone her own age. When I rebuffed her at the beginning, she had taken it in stride, but now she seemed distraught to see me with someone else. I looked forward to the end of the camp season when I would stop having to see her mope, especially at the end of the day when Diane came over to inquire how the day had gone.

"Maybe you should wait for me in your office," I said to Diane. "There's no sense in making Lucile suffer more than she has to."

"She'll get over it," Diane said.

"Every day she goes home brooding."

"That's part of her technique," Diane said. "She wants you to feel compassionate enough to look at her instead of me."

"You think she's faking?"

"I didn't say that. Nature is mysterious."

"I don't want to make her suffer."

"She'll survive."

Indeed, by the last day of camp Lucile had cheered up, and when she came over to say good-bye, she kissed me on the cheek.

"You'll remember me forever," she said. "I know it."

"I think you're right," I said.

"I know I am," she said and grinned as she walked away.

Daisy

$\mathscr{C}$OMING OUT OF the Morris Cohen Library, I ran into Daisy O'Connor, a recent acquaintance. Rick had introduced us.

"Hi," she greeted me. "I've been looking around for you."

"Well, here I am."

"Yeah, I thought it might be nice if we got together."

"All right, what can I do for you?"

"Well, that's very straightforward," she said. "I like that."

Totally befuddled and uncertain whether I had lost touch with reality, I needed to readjust my perceptions, especially my hearing. At Stephen's suggestion, I had just been in the music room, earphones to my head, listening to Dylan.

"You want to go out to a movie or something?" Daisy asked.

"You're asking me for a date?"

"No," she said, "it's not a date, just spend some time together."

"How's that different from a date?"

"A date is romantic," she said. "Getting together is something else."

"No sex, you mean."

"Well, I didn't say that either. Why don't we just take it one step at a time?"

"So going to the movies is the first step?"

"How about if you get me some grass?"

I imagined mowing the Great Lawn in front of Finley Hall to gather a few bags of grass for her. Did she own a pony or something?

"Weed," she said on seeing my puzzlement. Getting no response to that either, she added, "Marijuana."

"What makes you think I have any?" I said, surprised by her assumption.

"Well, don't you?"

"No," I said, "I don't even smoke tobacco."

"I thought since you hang out with Rick you were into it."

"What Rick does is his own business," I said. "We just happen to be classmates."

"All right," she said. "One can't always be right. See you around."

I watched her descend the library steps and head for Finley Hall. Only then, after having shooed her away, did her attractiveness register. The next time I saw her, I reminded her of her suggestion to go see a movie together.

"All right," she said, "as long as you know it's not a romantic date."

On Friday night, we went to see *A Hard Day's Night*, and afterward, we stopped for dinner at a restaurant on Macdougal Street. She insisted on paying her share to keep from obscuring the fact that we weren't dating. "I live nearby," I said as we left the restaurant. "You want go see my place?" I asked, expecting her to decline.

Taking my arm she said, "Lead the way." Yes, Daisy, totally different, didn't follow the same rules as everyone else, but she did have rules. "I have to tell you," she said on the way up the stairs to my place, "I don't go to bed with anyone on the first date."

"Well, I'll remember that when we go on our first date," I said.

"Oh, right," she said with a grin.

At my place, she continued very relaxed. "I guess you bring women here all the time," she said.

"No," I said, "you're only the second."

"Who was first?"

"Someone I met during the summer. She helped me find this place."

"And where is she now?"

"We don't see each other anymore. She was looking for a husband."

"You weren't ready to make a commitment, or you didn't want her?"

"Both, I guess."

"Good," she said. "I'm not ready for that either. I don't think I'll ever be."

"I know," I said, "you just want us to be friends."

"That's right," she said. "I don't get into entangled relationships."

"No commitments, you mean."

"Not long ones," she said.

We sat in my bedroom with only the kitchen light coming through the open door for atmosphere.

"I live with my mother," she said.

"And your father?"

"He ran off," she said nonchalantly, "and your parents?"

"They're still together, but they ought to get a divorce."

"It's always like that," she said.

"Not always," I said, but I wanted to change the subject. "What have you been up to?"

"I went to a nudist colony for the summer," she said.

I kept my gaze on the floor, glad that there wasn't enough light in the room for her to see my face.

"You're shocked," she said.

I couldn't tell whether my reaction amused or disappointed her. "I'm not," I said.

"Yes, you are. I can tell," she insisted.

"I'm only surprised," I said. "What was it like?"

"Quite an experience," she said. "I had a good time. I may go there next summer."

I shoved the summer into the distant future and decided not to think about it at the moment.

"I'm sorry I mentioned it," she said. "I didn't mean to upset you. It's no big deal, you know. Everybody knows what the human body looks like."

"That's right," I said.

She got up from the armchair and came over to where I was sitting on the windowsill. I stood up and she put her arms around my neck, bringing her nose to rub against mine. I tilted my head searching for her lips and, she having done the same, our teeth clicked. She laughed and squeezed to reassure me. "Nothing in the world is perfect," she whispered, "and it's still a wonderful world."

I kissed her again, and indeed the world was wonderful, but getting late, I remembered that we had agreed that she wouldn't spend the night with me on our first date, for what else could I now call it? "I'll take you home now if you're ready," I said.

"I've changed my mind," she said. "I'll stay tonight if you want me."

She woke me up very early in the morning. My eyes opened to gaze at her smile, as radiant as it had been the night before. "I have to go," she whispered.

"So early?"

"I want to get home before my mother wakes up."

Ah, another surprise. Did her mother know about the nudist camp, an interesting question? "All right," I said. "Let's first go out to breakfast."

"No," she said. "We'll do that some other time. I have to get home."

"All right," I said. "I'll take you."

"You don't have to," she said.

I insisted. We took the local up to 72nd Street, and I walked her up to 74th and Amsterdam. When we got to corner she said, "Let's say good-bye here, just in case."

"Your mother waits up for you?"

"One never knows," she said and laughed.

The next time we ran into each other on campus, she said to me,

"Listen, I did the wrong thing staying with you the other night. You need a regular girlfriend, and I'm not into that right now."

"All right," I said. "I'll wait until you're ready."

"That'll be a long wait," she said, "maybe forever. You can't wait for me. There are many other women around."

"Stay with me until I find someone else," I said half jokingly.

"That doesn't work," she said.

"I guess you're the one who needs someone else."

"Don't be silly," she said. "It's not that at all. How can I explain this to you? I'm not ready. If I let you think that I am, I'll hurt you too much. I don't want to hurt you at all, but if I hurt you a little now, that's better than later hurting you a lot. You see what I mean?"

"Good-bye then," I said.

"I'm not going anywhere," she said. "We'll both still be in school, and we have the same friends. We'll still see each other, so it's not good-bye."

"Right," I said.

But she had never sat with my friends in the cafeteria. She wasn't the conversational type, and being Rick's friend, she wasn't partial to Stephen.

A few weeks later, I made an excursion to the Upper East Side to visit Laura. She came to the door in her bathrobe, a cup of tea in her hand. "Oh, Mario, I'm so glad to see you,"

The front door led into the kitchen. To my surprise, at the sink, Daisy stood washing the dishes. "Hello, Mario," she said flashing her usual smile, which I no longer took credit for eliciting.

"You two know each other?" Laura inquired in a tone I interpreted as false.

"We're old friends," Daisy said.

"Well, good," Laura said. "Then no one can blame me for throwing the two of you together."

"Is our being in the same room something blameworthy?"

"That's not what I meant," Laura said in a tense voice and at the same time letting her body take on the semblance of being about to collapse.

"Oh, sit down," Daisy said moving away from the sink and taking Laura by the arm. "You shouldn't stress yourself out in your condition."

"What condition is that?" I inquired wondering whether Daisy had noticed Laura's acting talent often used to portray an ill person.

"She's totally run down," Daisy said. "She needs rest."

"I do need to lie down," Laura said.

"We'll help you to the bedroom," Daisy said. "Mario, you take her other arm."

The situation was too ridiculous to take seriously. However, in no position to say so, I went along with Daisy's suggestion. I offered my arm as another crutch for Laura and helped her to the bedroom. Pretending to be relieved, she curled into the bed and said, "I think I need a nap."

"All right, we'll go back to the kitchen and be quiet," Daisy said. Taking me by the hand, she lead the retreat. In the kitchen, she continued washing the dishes and putting everything away.

"Were you hired as a housekeeper?" I inquired wondering whether Laura's performance had indeed fooled Daisy. Looking into her eyes, I determined that she really believed that Laura was ill. I did note an illness in Laura, but my diagnosis indicated something other than physical. Seeing the futility of explaining that to Daisy, I let it go.

"Are you going to mop the floor also?" I asked.

"Not right now," she said. "I'm tired, and I need a shower. I think I'll take one if you don't mind."

The bathtub occupied part of the kitchen, just like at my place.

"Not at all," I said. "I'll go sit in the living room."

Laura's apartment was a railroad flat. To get to the living room, I would have to walk through the bedroom.

"No," she said, "you'll wake up Laura. You don't have to go anywhere."

She began to undress, and I wondered whether she expected me to look the other way. I merely gazed at her as she silently disrobed. She smiled at me and turned to adjust the flow before climbing into the tub. I sat still for a while listening to the cascading water, then I got up, walked to the front door, and left without a word.

Bonnie

ABOUT NINE O'CLOCK in the evening, Bonnie knocked on my door. The day before, we had sat on the Great Lawn in front of Finley Hall, and she had laid back to rest her head on my lap. Then, she asked if I would put her up for one night. She was going away for the weekend, and she had to get to the Port Authority bus terminal early the next day. She would rather not have to come in from New Hyde Park so early in the morning.

"Here I am," she said nervously when I opened the door. She held a small traveling bag. "Where should I put this?" she asked.

"Oh, anywhere," I said. "Make yourself at home."

Gingerly, she peered into the bedroom on her right. On the wall over the bed hung a poster-size picture of Karl Marx and on the adjacent wall another poster called "Young Venus," a nude Asian girl standing up to her knees in water. Bonnie glanced around and then walked across the kitchen and inspected the other room, only a bed and a dresser in that one. The room reminded her of a vestigial limb, she said. She left her bag by the dresser and returned to the kitchen.

"Would you like some dinner?" I asked.

"I already ate," she answered, "but how about some coffee?"

"Coming up," I said.

Cold coffee in the pot already, I lit the stove and place the pot on the burner. She sat down at the table and reached for the cigarettes in her purse.

"What a clean ashtray," she remarked as she slid it closer to herself from the side of the table against the wall. She crossed her legs and tried to strike a sophisticated pose as she smoked. Extremely thin, her hair very short, her face pleasant in an unusual way, cute rather than pretty, reminded me of an acorn. Her thinness made her seem frail and very young.

I poured two cups of coffee, and I sat down. "So where is it you're going tomorrow?" I asked.

"I'm going to stay at this dude ranch for the weekend. This guy whose father owns it invited me. My parents know them, so they're letting me go. You don't know how glad I am to get away for a couple of days."

"I can imagine," I said.

She sipped the coffee between puffs of her cigarette.

"You know what they would do to me if they knew I was here in your apartment?"

"They would disinherit you," I mockingly said.

"They would kill me," she said crushing into the ashtray the remnants of her cigarette. "They would kill me," she repeated. "Can I use your phone? I have to call home before it gets too late."

"The phone is in there," I said pointing to the room she had first inspected, "on the desk."

She lit another cigarette, and taking the ashtray with her, she went to make the call. I stayed at the table and heard the clicking as she dialed the ten numbers.

"Hello, Mama," she said, ". . .Yes, I'm at Karen's. . . yes, I just got here. . . My dance lesson went well today. . . Yes, it went especially well today. . . The bus leaves at seven tomorrow. . . Yeah, I'll call you. . . I wouldn't want to drive there by myself. I'm better off taking the bus. . . I'm all right here at Karen's. . . She doesn't mind, Mama. . . Yeah, I'll be on my best behavior. . . Tuna fish, I had a tuna fish sandwich. . . It was a good place. I know the place. . . Very clean, it's a very clean place. . . No, they wouldn't keep tuna fish salad from one day to another. . . I know, Mama. Nothing's as good as eating home. . . You're right. You can't be too careful these days. . . What did you have for dinner?. . . Aha. . . Yeah. . . That sounds good. . . Oh, he always complains. . . No matter how good the food is, he always finds something to complain about. . . Yeah, I understand. . . Sure. . . No, no, you're right. . . of course. There's always room for improvement.

. . Yeah, that's life. . . You have to take the good with the bad. . . All right, Mama, I'm going to hang up. This is a long distance call. . . Yeah, say good night to Dad. . . Mama, I understand. . . Yeah, good night. . . I'll call you first thing when I get there. . . Good night, Mama." She hung up and took a long drag on the cigarette.

She sat on the bed and looked around the room again. "This is a real cozy place you have here," she said.

"I like it," I said.

"I almost didn't get here," she went on. "This place is hard to find. I did follow your directions," she paused, "but it's creepy down here. The streets are deserted. Nobody lives down here."

"It's sort of nice that way," I said. "During the week, everybody leaves at five o'clock, so it's quiet at night, and on the weekends it's quiet all day."

"It's too quiet for the city," she said.

"It's only a short walk to Washington Square," I said. "There, you can get all the noise you want."

"I'd be afraid to take a walk," she said.

"It's safe. This is one of the safest areas in the city, absolutely no street crime."

A loud noise came from the apartment above, something being thrown across the room, then the sound of voices arguing.

"That's Mike and Cynthia," I said. "They fight all the time."

The ceiling shook with another loud thump, like a heavy piece of furniture falling.

"It sounds serious," Bonnie said.

"Nah, they fight all the time. Mike is a truck driver for the post office."

"What if he hurts her?"

"Mike is a woman," I said.

"And Cynthia?"

"Cynthia too."

"Do they hurt each other?"

"Nah, not usually. Cynthia has a black eye once in a while, but that's as bad as it gets."

The noise continued. Bonnie had finished her second cigarette and had lit a third.

"What do they fight about?"

"I don't know," I said. "I guess Mike is jealous. There's this pimp on the fifth floor. He's been making passes at Cynthia. Maybe they're fighting about that. A few days ago Mike and Carlino, the pimp, had an argument right out in the street."

"This street?"

"Yeah, right here in front of the building. Carlino pulled a knife on Mike."

"Good God! A knife?"

"Nobody got hurt," I assured her.

"God, is there anybody normal in this building?"

"Yeah, me," I said.

"What's that?" she exclaimed, pointing at the desk, a bug crawled across the green ink blotter.

"It's a roach," I said. With my hand I swept it to the floor and stepped on it, the operation swift and accurate. For a few seconds she sat motionless as if she had witnessed a daring exploit.

"What's the matter, you've never seen a roach before?"

"I've seen roaches," she said defensively. "I just don't like them. Are there lots of them here?"

"A few," I said. "I breed them and sell them to pet shops."

"Very funny," she grimaced. "Really, I mean, they won't crawl on you when you're sleeping?"

"Nah," I said. "They've better things to do at night."

She blushed a little as she flicked ashes into the ashtray she had placed on her lap. Emotionally drained, she momentarily became silent. "I'm sorry," she said trying to recover.

"For what?"

"The way I reacted to the roach. You're not upset, are you?"

78

"Nah," I said.

"I like your apartment. At least it's yours. I wish I had my own place away from my parents."

"You can, if you want to."

"No, it's too much for me."

Her parents cared more about money and appearances, she explained to me. She loathed the kind of life they led. I tried to imagine the people she described, and I nodded in polite commiseration.

"If it's so bad, why don't you just leave them?"

"Where would I go? What would I do? I have no money."

"I don't have money either."

"It's different, you're a man."

"I guess that makes a difference," I said.

"Hey, where's the john?" she asked.

"Out in the hall," I pointed to the door.

"Out there?"

"Yeah, the first door on the left, across from the stairs," I said as she got up to go. "It's locked. Take the key, right there hanging on that nail by the door."

She reached for the key, and having obtained it, opened the door and stuck her head out to scout the hallway. Convinced that the coast was clear, she gave me an apologetic smile and slipped out, making sure that the door didn't slam shut. I listened as she struggled with the lock on the toilet room door. The key didn't always fit just right. I decided to give her time to work it out before offering assistance, but there was no need. She managed. Shortly, I heard her come out of the bathroom and speak to someone.

"I met an old lady out there," she said when she came back. "She asked me who I was."

"Don't mind her," I said.

"She was nice enough."

"She's a pain in the ass—always sticking her nose in other people's business."

The old lady lived down the hall, and across from her, Robert, a telephone installer addicted to heroin.

"Are you in there, Mario?" I heard Chuck's voice from the hallway.

"Yeah, I'm here."

Bedecked in cowboy boots, dungarees, and a red, white, and blue suede vest over a T-shirt—what looked like an escapee from Buffalo Bill's Wild West show walked in. His blond hair falling over his shoulders, his moustache worthy of its model, this imitator of the legendary showman was my downstairs neighbor.

"I got this dynamite stuff. You wanna buy?"

"Nah," I said. "I got plenty."

"Not like this."

"No thanks."

"I also got some acid, first rate."

"Nah," I said, "not buying today."

"Okay, but it's gonna be gone by tomorrow."

"This is Bonnie," I said.

"Hi," he gave her the once over, unimpressed. "You wanna buy some grass?" he asked, not really expecting to be taken up.

"No," she timidly said.

Chuck crossed the room and sat on the windowsill. He looked out the window long enough to create the impression that perhaps he was going to do just that and nothing else. Bonnie's nerves frayed by the presence of a third person, she looked at me for some clue as to what Chuck was up to, but she got none. I knew that he would leave after making some futile attempt at conversation, usually in spurts.

Finally he said, "I'm going to knock a wall out of my apartment, make it two rooms instead of three." He spoke still looking through the window at the lack of activity in the street. He then turned his eyes into the room. Unable to focus on anything, he looked neither at Bonnie nor at me.

"Sounds like a big job," I said.

"Nah," he said, "take a sledgehammer, one, two, three, no problem."

Chuck looked back into the street. A taxi had stopped in front of the building, and two women got out.

"They always come in a taxi," Chuck said.

"Who?"

"Those sluts from the fifth floor. You ever been up there?"

"Nah," I said.

"You haven't missed anything."

"You go up there?" Bonnie asked him in turn.

"Once," he said. "I looked in just to see what was going on, but it was too disgusting. The whole apartment stinks. I don't think they ever clean up. You know, they all sleep in one bed."

"How many are there?"

"All depends, sometimes more, sometimes less. There's about four of them now."

"Four women?"

"Yeah, sometimes he's got boys up there too. Never seen anything like that since Vietnam. Merchant marine, you know, just take the stuff there and come back," he said as if to explain that he wasn't fool enough to be in the military. "But it's something else over there, if you know what I mean."

"I don't know," Bonnie said.

"Well, it's this way, you see, they give you this pistol for when you go ashore, you know. You carry it around in a holster. Once, I got in this rickshaw. You know what a rickshaw is?"

"Sure, I know."

"Well, you see, you tell the gook, 'Take me here, take me there,' and if he don't want to take you, you take out the pistol. He takes you."

Neither Bonnie nor I commented on that. Chuck resumed his aimless gazing, and then got up as if to leave, but he remembered why he had come up.

"Do you know if these walls between the rooms are supporting walls?" he asked.

"Nah, man, I don't know," I said.

"I gotta check that out," he said.

"Yeah, you better do that."

"Funny if your whole kitchen fell in on me, no?" he said as he backed into the hall.

I got up and locked the door.

"That's a strange person," Bonnie said.

"Yeah," I said, "I guess so."

"I gotta get up early tomorrow. I should go to bed soon. Where do I wash up?"

"Right there in the sink," I said. "If you want to take a shower, the tub is right next to it."

She went over to the closet-like compartment and drew the blue shower curtain to reveal a small tub. "This is absolutely cute," she said, and she went to get her night bag.

She performed her ablutions then donned a pink flannel nightgown. All the while, I pretended to be busy going through some papers on my desk. She came to the door of the room and said, "I need sheets for the bed."

"Sleep in this bed with me," I suggested. "It doesn't make sense for you to sleep over there and me over here."

She retrieved a pack of cigarettes from the pocket of her nightgown, took one out and lit it. She then took a long puff and pretended to think the matter over. I could tell that she had already made up her mind.

"Well, I don't know," she said.

I reached out and taking her hand pulled her to me. She didn't resist. She sat on my lap. She was much lighter than I anticipated. She felt wiry and angular. She sat still, one hand on my shoulder, the other holding the cigarette. She seemed perplexed, not quite sure how she should behave.

"This is not what I had in mind when I came here," she said. "I just needed a place to stay tonight."

"I know," I said, "but now that you're here we might as well."

"Are you sure you want me to sleep with you?"

"I'm sure," I said, although less certain than I had been before she had been on my lap.

"I did ask you if you had an extra bed, and you said you did. I don't want you to think that I came here wanting to sleep with you."

"I don't think that," I said. "Why would I think that?"

She stood up, and I went to the kitchen to wash up. When I came back, she was sitting on the bed, her back against the wall and her knees drawn toward her chest, the ashtray next to her replete with butts.

"Stop smoking, will ya? The whole room is full of smoke."

"I can't stop," she said. "I'm too tense. I got to tell you something."

"Yeah?"

"Well, it's like this," she paused to inhale.

I unbuttoned my shirt as I waited for her revelation.

"You see. . .," she said, and paused, hoping that I would finish the sentence.

I threw my shirt on the desk and remained silent as I began to untie my shoelaces.

"I never slept with anyone," she blurted.

"Well, don't worry about it," I said. I took off my pants and placed them on the desk beside the shirt.

"I'm not worried," she said. "I just thought I ought to tell you."

"I'm glad you told me," I said trying to make her feel more at ease.

She showed no inclination to move from her sitting position or to stop smoking.

"You're not going to bed with that on, are you?" I asked.

"With what?"

"That nightgown."

"I always sleep in it."

"Oh, take it off."

She got up and pulled the nightgown over her head. "These too?" she asked putting her hands on the elastic of her underpants.

I nodded affirmatively. Once in bed, after a while of caressing her, my hand went down to her clit and then a little further in.

"Don't do that," she whispered.

"Why not?"

"You might go in too far."

"How far is that?"

"You might break the hymen."

"So what?"

"I'd be in trouble then. My parents might find out."

"What are you talking about?"

"The doctor might tell them."

"They have you examined?"

She didn't answer.

"You're all crazy," I said.

"I don't want to take a chance," she said.

"Your hymen is probably broken already."

"I'm a virgin," she reaffirmed.

"You use Tampax, don't you?"

"You think that could do it?"

"Of course," I said.

She was silent for a moment, then she said, "I don't want to take a chance anyway."

"Suit yourself," I said.

"Are you angry at me?"

"No," I said.

"Yes, you are. I can tell."

"I'm not angry," I said turning to hold her.

"I knew this would happen," she said. "Are we still friends?"

"Of course we are."

"I need a cigarette," she said.

She got up to get the cigarettes and the ashtray. She came back to bed and smoked for a long time. I watched the glow of the cigarette rise and fall as she alternately rested her hand on her knee then brought the cigarette to her lips. Finally I dozed off.

It was a gray chilly morning and drizzling by the time Bonnie left for the bus terminal. I watched her from the window as she, suitcase in hand, crossed the street and disappeared around the corner.

Orphans

I MET HARRY in World History 101. He was an amiable guy, very slim and always dressed in what I then considered conservative attire. I was into denim work shirts and dungarees. He always wore a white shirt and dress pants to class. At the time, that was odd for a City College student, or at least to those of us who hung out in Finley Hall. I never really mixed with the North Campus crowd, so about them there's not much I can say, other than they were conservatives. From his looks, I would have placed Harry with them, but he turned out to be all right.

He, and also his wife, Ellen, grew up in an orphanage. When they reached college age they married and enrolled at the City University. His friend Robert, another orphanage alumnus, was also married, but his wife was not from the orphanage. The four of them were a closely knit group, but they were trying to expand. I became one of their new recruits.

For someone her age, Ellen was very motherly, something rare in college women. But perhaps I'm wrong about that. Leslie, who had introduced me to my close friend, Stephen, had a very motherly approach to dealing with him. The difference, I guess, was that Leslie had a very "in" look that, back then, didn't go along with the word "motherly." Ellen, on the other hand, at least in her attire, was just as conservative as her husband. She had a bubbly personality and a zaftig body.

Still, her most salient characteristic was her motherly attitude toward men in general. When they invited me to their place, she was very solicitous. She constantly asked me whether I needed this or that. Was I comfortable where I sat? Did I need another drink? Did I want a pillow to lean on? When I sat in the rocking chair, she offered to stand behind it and rock me. I found that rather charming.

The next time I ran into Harry on campus, he invited me to lunch at a neighborhood restaurant. I took that as a continuation of friendly overtures. At the restaurant, however, he became rather unpleasant by continually proposing riddles and logic games to which he knew the answers, but I had to struggle to figure them out. Seeking solutions to inane games was not my idea of a pleasant pastime. Our parting that day was less than cordial.

A few weeks later, after my last class for the day, I ran into his friend, Robert.

"Come up to my place tonight. We can take a ride in my car. It's being tuned up, and I'm picking it up on my way home."

"From my place to yours is a long trip," I said. Robert lived in Washington Heights.

"Come up with me right now," he suggested.

"Well, I don't know," I said, but after mulling it over for a few seconds, I decided to accept his invitation.

Once off the subway, we went over to the auto shop where his Oldsmobile was undergoing repair. The place reeked of motor oil. Tito, the mechanic, surfaced from under the car, his face and arms covered with grease.

"How's it going?" Robert asked.

"You got more problems than I first thought," Tito said with a slight Puerto Rican accent.

"Will it be ready today?" Robert inquired. "I might need it tonight."

"Maybe," Tito said. "Check back at six o'clock. I'll tell you then. But I can tell you right now; you should get rid of this car. Fixing it costs more than buying a new one."

"Yeah, well, I'm thinking about it," Robert said.

As we walked out to the street, he looked despondent. "I can't get rid of the car," he said. "If I don't have a car, Stephanie will leave me."

"You're kidding me, right?"

"Nah, I wouldn't lie about that."

"You're not making sense. If she married for a car, she could've done much better than that one."

"Strange, right? You never can tell what's going on in a woman's head."

"I can't tell what's going in yours."

"Believe me I know her."

"I suppose you do," I conceded.

He soon bounced back. At the liquor store, he picked out a bottle of Retsina. "You're going to like this. It has an unusual taste," he said.

When we got to his place, his wife, Stephanie, was already preparing dinner. Robert kept me in the living room as he tried to convince me that Motown was the greatest sound ever and the Supremes the best women vocalists in the world. "It's sheer poetry," Robert said. "You ought to know. You write poetry, don't you?"

I didn't want to discuss poetry with Robert. "Maybe we ought to see if Stephanie needs help," I said.

"Nah," Robert said, "we'll just get in her way."

"Are you sure?"

"Yeah, she throws me out all the time."

"Out of the kitchen?"

"Yeah, she doesn't throw me out of bed. That's for sure," he said. A forced laugh followed, then an uncomfortable silence before getting back to talking about music.

Several times, Stephanie emerged from the kitchen to sit with us and then retreated back into the kitchen to check on the cooking. She seemed comfortable enough doing all the work. The other guests arrived. Harry and Ellen brought along Judy, another friend of theirs, and with three women in the place, I figured I could forget about the kitchen. I also reminded myself not to sit too close to Ellen, and I limited all my interaction with her, having concluded that the restaurant incident was Harry's reaction to the attention I had received from his wife when I had been at their place.

At six o'clock, Robert called the garage to find out how the repair on his car had progressed. To his delight, the car was ready, and he could pick it up if he got there before Tito left for the day. "Sure," Robert said and dashed out to retrieve his car.

The Retsina became more palatable as the evening progressed.

"We should drive out to the cemetery tonight," Harry said.

"To where?" I inquired thinking that I had misheard what he said.

"To a cemetery," Harry repeated. "Haven't you ever done that? Drinking a bottle of wine in a cemetery is quite an experience, really ghoulish fun."

I looked around to see whether Harry was kidding, but everyone else seemed to be at ease with the idea.

Taking the suggestion as a joke, I said, "You can go without me."

"We don't have to decide that right now," Ellen said. "The night is young."

"Cemeteries are locked at night."

"Of course, we have to climb the fence," Harry said.

"That's right, the women have to wear pants."

"Or the men have to go first."

"They can't go first; they have to help the us over the fence."

"It's too dark to see anything anyway."

"Oh, good, I don't have to put on pants," Stephanie said.

"Or take them off," Robert quipped.

After a couple of bottles of wine the question of driving out to the cemetery came up again.

"Are we going down to the cemetery or not?"

"You mean up to the cemetery."

"You're joking, right?"

"No, let's go. Might as well use the car while it still works."

"Bring the wine."

I had only been to a cemetery once before, as a child, to visit my grandmother's grave. I remembered my mother saying, "I was only fourteen when she died." "Are you going to die when I'm fourteen?" I asked her. "Don't be silly," she said bending down to hold me. "You'll be an old man before I die." Fourteen, at that moment, had seemed to me close to old age.

We all crammed into Robert's Oldsmobile and drove across University Heights Bridge to the Bronx. We parked on a deserted part of Woodlawn Avenue between Van Cortlandt Park and Woodlawn Cemetery.

"You go over first," Robert said to Harry when we got to the cemetery fence. "I'll boost the girls up on this side, and you help them climb down on the other."

"Okay," Harry said, "give me a boost."

Robert locked his fingers together to provide a step for Harry, who reached up to pull himself over the iron fence and then leaped to the ground on the other side. I stood back wondering why I was going along with this silly venture.

When I was a boy, I often climbed over the high wire fence in back of the apartment building into the empty lot that was fenced off. The children on the block used it as a park. Mostly we got in through holes in the fence, but when they were patched, climbing over the fence became routine. One day, I ripped my pants as I swung over the top. Iris Rivera, the block blond, was looking up as I descended. "I see all the way up your leg," she shouted laughing as if she were having the time of her life. "You don't see nothing," I said knowing full well that only my pants had ripped. I was more concerned about what would happen when I got home after having damaged something that would cost money to replace.

Once the three women got over the fence, Robert gave me a boost. Then, he had to pull himself up on his own.

"We'll have to do the same thing on the way out," I said.

"I'll climb out first," Robert said.

"Right," Stephanie agreed.

It was too dark to see the expression on her face, and the tone of her voice was impossible to interpret.

"Let's find a place to sit and drink the wine."

"We're not sitting on graves, are we?"

"We just lean on the stones, that's all."

The married people sat next to each other and that left me with Judy. Having dismissed the idea that my friends were trying to set us up, I had paid little attention to her until then.

"Let's sit by the mausoleum over there," Robert said pointing to the large stone structure.

We passed the wine around, and everyone drank straight from the bottle. No one had remembered to bring cups.

"Let's change partners," Stephanie said.

"For what? We're not dancing."

"For sitting partners, that's all," she said.

"I think my wife's drunk already," Robert said. "Let's go home."

"Let's," she said.

"Let's finish the bottle," Harry said.

"All right," Robert said, "one more round will do it."

"At least the wine is good," Ellen said.

"It's good enough," Judy said.

"Better than anything else," Stephanie put in.

On the way home Robert offered to drive Harry and Ellen down to their place, so they wouldn't have to take the subway. He would take Judy too. She lived near them.

"I'm too tired to be riding around town," Stephanie said.

"I'll drop you off first," Robert suggested.

"I can't be home all alone. You know I get scared at night," she said, annoyed that Robert was ignoring her phobia.

"Mario, will you stay with her for a little while? I'll be right back."

"Sure," I said, "if it's all right with Stephanie."

"Fine," she said in a vague tone, her mood indecipherable.

Robert dropped us off in front of his building, and I went up with Stephanie. Once in the apartment, she poured me another glass of wine. "I'm cold," she said, and she left the room to fetch a blanket. She returned with the blanket wrapped over her shoulders, and she sat on the couch to watch me drink the wine. After a few minutes, she opened the blanket and gestured to me to come sit next to her. I pretended not to notice the invitation.

"Is there something wrong with your eyesight?" she asked.

"What do you mean?" I continued to feign.

"Come sit next to me," she said.

"I'm all right where I am," I said.

"You'll be better off here."

"What about Robert?"

"He's not here," she said in an angry tone. "He left on purpose to give you this chance. Take it."

"I don't think he'd do that."

"Okay, you're right, but what about me? I'm making you an offer, and it's not right for you to refuse it. It's kind of an insult. I don't deserve to be insulted. Do I?"

"Put yourself in my place."

"Put yourself in mine."

"I get rejected often enough," I said.

"That's not what I'm talking about," she retorted.

"What then?"

"Oh, forget it," she said. "Have another drink."

She sat there glaring at me until Robert returned.

Silver Spurs

RICK HAD DROPPED out of school, married, then resumed his intellectual pursuits. When I met him, he was back at City College. A career as a writer beckoned him, he said. I suggested that he go to Paris and hang out on the Left Bank. But life at the college was exciting enough for him, and that soon led to marital problems. One day I ran into him on the steps of Finley Hall.

"Mario, you have to help me," he pleaded. "My wife locked me out."

"I thought you had left her."

"I did, but it was a mistake. I want her back, but she won't even talk to me on the phone. If I could see her just once, I know I can explain everything."

How much understanding could he expect from an abandoned wife? I figured nothing much would help him with his marriage at that point.

"She goes to a bar on the East Side," he said. "She might be there tonight. Maybe I'll run into her, but I don't want to wait around alone. Come with me."

We got to the bar at seven, and Rick droned on about Carolyn. He drank and kept an eye on the door. By nine-thirty she had not arrived.

"She's not going to show up," I said.

"Still early," Rick said. "Have another drink."

I had nursed a beer for the last hour. In contrast, Rick had been making a significant contribution to the bar's gross. Two young women sat at the next table. Rick engaged them in conversation, but they soon noticed that he was drunk and lost interest. All the same to me, having expected nothing from the excursion but a couple of beers.

"Are you going to manage taking your friend home?" the barmaid asked me at one o'clock.

"I may need some help. You want to come along?"

She smiled shaking her head. I appreciated her compact look. I watched her turn away to clear a neighboring table, and I wished that I had been less flippant with her. I managed to get Rick on his feet and guided him to the door. Once out of the bar, the evening continued on a downward spiral. We took the cross-town bus then the subway down to Chelsea.

Out on the street, I had trouble keeping him on his feet. "Oh, fuck!" I exclaimed, but Rick was so out of it that there was no way to get across to him that he was putting some strain on me.

He plopped down on a stoop and tried to curl up. "You can't lie here," I said.

"Mario!" he called out.

"I'm here," I said.

"Don't leave me, Mario. I can't make it alone."

"I'm not leaving you."

"The bitch didn't show up, but it's okay. I'm to blame. It was my fault, but I still love her."

"Rick, we're almost there. Come on now, make a little effort, and we'll get there," I said. I put one arm around his middle, and with the other, I held his arm in place over my shoulder, but his weight was too much for me to haul without cooperation.

"I can't see in this fog."

"What fog? It's all in your mind," I said.

"Hey, you know, we should've picked up those chicks at the bar. We could've got laid."

Eventually, we got to his building and faced another set of steps. "Come on, we have to get up the stairs," I urged him. By that time he had lost all interest in the upward direction. "Come on, just a few more steps," I cajoled. We were almost at the top of the landing, the door to his place visible. I made another gargantuan effort, but he sat down on the steps. "Give me the key," I said.

Half asleep, he didn't seem to understand. I stifled the impulse to slap him awake. Instead, I delved into his pockets until I found his key chain. I was trying to determine which key fit the front lock when the door opened slightly. Shit, I thought, the wrong door, and I'll have to deal with an irate neighbor.

A young woman undid the door chain and came out into the hallway.

"My God, what's happened to him?" She asked more in disgust than inquiry.

I succumbed to a fit of discretion and, waiting for her to explain her presence, merely stared at her.

"Let's get him inside," she said.

Glad to get help, I followed her instructions; we each took one side and tried to lift the slumping drunk to his feet.

"God, he stinks," she said.

"He got sick on the way home."

"Must have been some party," she smirked.

"Nah, he was just looking for his wife."

"Was he?"

We dragged him over to the bed and plopped him down. He curled up into it, shoes and all. The major task for the evening completed, I found myself at loose ends.

The question of the woman's identity began to gnaw at me. I wasn't sure whether I had deposited Rick in his own bed or someone else's. For some unexplainable reason, perhaps her self-assured look, I felt reluctant to question her. She noticed my uneasiness and let me squirm a bit. Finally she said, "I'm Carolyn."

"You're his wife!" I exclaimed. "You were here all along."

"Ain't that a bitch?" she said.

"Poor Rick!"

"Poor you," she countered.

I realized I had not introduced myself, and I made amends.

"So what else are you doing tonight, Mario?"

"I had enough doing for one night," I said.

95

"Come home with me," she said. "I get lonely in bed by myself."

"I can't do that," I said. "Rick's my friend."

"Well," she said, "you can think it over while you walk me to my car."

I agreed to that. Before we left, we took Rick's shoes off and covered him with a blanket. Then I followed Carolyn down the stairs, all the while wondering whether she heard the jingling of my silver spurs.

Yesterday

D'Anuncio

SOMETIMES I HEARD noise through the kitchen side door that led to the building's supposed storage room. In the daytime, I figured Charlie, the maintenance guy, was taking things in and out through the hallway entrance. Generally, the clanking wasn't too annoying, and I put up with it, but one noisy morning I went down to D'Anuncio's place to complain. D'Anuncio was the landlord's agent. He collected the monthly rent, and he took care of renting the apartments when they became vacant. With the tenants, he always tried to be accommodating.

"Well, of course," he attempted to explain to me, "Charlie has to get the mop and pail when he cleans the stairway, that's all. Is he making too much noise? I'll talk to him. I'll tell him to be as quiet as possible."

Over his shoulder, I saw a typewriter and a stack of paper on his table. "You're writing a book?"

"Yeah," he said, "I spent the advance already. Now I have to produce."

He saw that the word "advance" impressed me, so he proceeded to tell me about the book. "It's about organized crime, you know, the Mafia."

"A novel?"

"Oh, no, it's the real thing. None of it is fiction."

"So how do you do your research?"

He took out a cigarette and brought it up to his lips. I watched him light the match and laboriously try to make it reach the cigarette. After a puff, he said, "Oh, I know people."

I waited for him to tell me more, but he only kept puffing on his cigarette. Maybe trying to determine whether he could divulge information about his contacts, he stared into my eyes. "Well, you can read everything when the book comes out," he said.

At the moment, I was more concerned with Charlie's use of the room adjacent to my kitchen. When I first saw Charlie, an old white-haired man, mopping the place, I knew D'Anuncio was getting the help at a bargain price. Whenever I passed Charlie in the stairway, I heard him mumbling in Italian. I assumed he didn't speak a word of English. Out front, the hatchway to the basement open, I often saw him sitting on the iron steps, liquor bottle in hand.

Late at night, I kept hearing noise through the door between my kitchen and the storage room. Why anyone would be in there in the middle of the night became the question. The fact that there was a door between my apartment and the storage room began to gnaw on me, so I dropped a note to the City Department of Buildings to check exactly what they had down as my rental space. In a few weeks, I got a response. According to their records, I was renting a three-room apartment. I went down to see D'Anuncio.

"Well, I had no idea," he said. "I'll have to bring it up with the landlord, Mr. DeAngelis. He didn't tell me anything about your apartment being three rooms."

"Well, I'm paying rent for three rooms and getting only two. You better tell him that I'm in touch with the Housing Department."

A couple of days later, D'Anuncio knocked on my door. "I worked it all out for you," he said. "We're moving everything out of that room, and you can have it."

"Well, thanks," I said, wondering why he thought he was doing me a favor. "You know, you've been using my room for months. You owe me rent."

"Well, that's all together another matter. Like I said before, I knew nothing about this being a three-room apartment. I was as bamboozled as you. On that issue, you have to deal directly with DeAngelis."

"I may do that," I said.

"Well, do what you think is best. Right now you're ahead, and it's always best to quit while you're ahead. That's what I think, but you do whatever you have to."

"Okay, thanks again for helping me out."

"Sure," he said. "I'm always glad to do the right thing. Oh, another thing, there's a bed in there. You can have it for five bucks, if you want it. Otherwise I'll have to move it out."

I should've claimed the bed for part of the rent DeAngelis owed me, but I figured D'Anuncio needed the five bucks. So, I gave him the money, and I had the extra room with a bed I didn't need.

A few days later, I ran into Charlie mopping the hallway, and he raised his voice as I went by. A bunch of Italian words rolled out of his mouth in a tone I knew to be reserved for expletives. I figured he was cursing me out, and the best way to deal with the situation was to ignore him. Whether I ran into him in the hallway or outside as he sat drinking by the hatchway, his cursing at me became a routine.

I ran into D'Anuncio a few weeks later.

"How's your writing coming along?" I asked him.

"Oh, I'm getting there," he said. "I'm doing more research. That's the hard part."

"Yeah? I always thought that was the easy part of writing a book."

"Not with this kind of book. It's not like sitting in the public library looking things up. This is very different."

"So, you're doing field work?"

"I suppose you can call it that."

"Well, good luck."

"I need luck," he said.

A large key chain hung from his belt, and the multiple keys jingled as he walked up the steps. The physical ailment that affected his hands, always noticeable when he smoked, included other parts of his body. It made his walking slow and jerky, and the sound of the keys on the chain evoked the image of disability after he was out of sight.

As I got home from work one day, an ambulance was pulling away. The sun, part way behind the low warehouse buildings, shone on the glass windows painted opaque to keep the light off the storage floors. Two cops, about to climb back into their patrol car, were talking to my neighbor, Chuck. I heard one of them say, "This happens all the time. He was an old man."

I watched the patrol car back out onto Spring Street.

"Hey, Mario, wait up," Chuck called out when he saw me.

"What's up?"

"Oh, man, Charlie did himself in."

"What are you talking about?"

"He fell down the basement steps, broke his neck."

"That's awful," I said, thinking that perhaps my having reclaimed my room had something to do with the accident.

"Can't be drinking all the time when you're that old, know what I mean? I tried turning him on to grass, but he wasn't interested."

"You think he'd still be alive if he'd only listened to you."

"Probably! I got some good stuff. Let me know if you want any."

"Yeah, I'll let you know," I said. "If you're still around when my hair turns white."

"How about your old lady, she want any?"

"She doesn't smoke either."

"She can bake brownies," he said.

I looked into his face trying to figure out whether he was joking. He looked serious.

After a while, I didn't see D'Anuncio anymore. DeAngelis, the landlord, himself came by to collect the rent and to do the exterminating that didn't do any good anyway. The roaches kept coming back, and I got used to them. DeAngelis became the problem; he would invade the apartment whether or not I was there. Now and then, I would get home to the smell of insect spray. I would open the kitchen cabinets, and I knew he had sprayed into them regardless of their content. Several times I had to throw away food I suspected of being contaminated. Finally, I said to him, "Don't come into the apartment when I'm not here. You know that's the law."

"All right," he said. "But you have to let me in at least once a month to spray."

"Fine," I said, "but you know it doesn't do any good. The bugs come over from the warehouses."

"You're right," he said. "Still, I have to spray."

In a way, he had a good attitude. Most landlords didn't care about the infestation. Still, I didn't want him in the apartment in my absence, but he didn't listen. A week later, I got home to the smell of the spray all over the kitchen. I rushed to the hardware store on Bleecker Street, and I bought a lock to replace the one on the front door. I figured that would keep DeAngelis out, unless he knew how to pick the lock. The next time I ran into him I thought he would say something about being kept out, but he didn't mention it.

He lived across the river. "How's life in New Jersey?" I asked him.

"Boring," he said. "That's why I come over here and look after the building. Gives me something to do." He had been a construction worker, injured on the job, something to do with his spinal cord. He couldn't do heavy work anymore.

"So you took away D'Anuncio's job?"

"He left it behind."

"You mean he moved on?"

"Sort of. He was found dead in some abandoned building, shot in the head."

"Jesus!" I said. "A mugging?"

"I don't think so. He still had his wallet on him, nothing missing."

"Damn," I said. "What did you do with his manuscript?"

"What are you talking about?"

"He was writing a book," I said.

"Well, I don't know anything about that. He had no family,

so I donated all his stuff to the Salvation Army. I didn't see any manuscript."

"Shit," I said. "It could've been a best seller."

The Employment Service

AT A COMMUNITY CENTER in the South Bronx, I worked for the Employment Service, a branch of the Federal Labor Department. We occupied a whole floor, and a variety of other public service organizations took up the rest of the building.

Lydia Sotomajor Schmidt was the only Puerto Rican female interviewer in the Bronx office.

"You're wondering how I got the name Schmidt," she said to me when we first met.

"It's an interesting name for a Puerto Rican," I conceded.

"I'm not officially dropping it," she said, "but you can call me Sotomajor, if you wish."

"What if I just call you Lydia?"

"That's fine too," she grinned.

Most of us spoke Spanish, but for a long while I labored under the impression that Betty Green lacked the language. She was a group supervisor acting as temporary office manager until a permanent one could be found. A nervous little woman, who rode in from White Plains every morning to do her missionary work in the South Bronx, her hands always caressing each other, her lips slightly pouting, she looked like a bird with a small beak. She took her job seriously and tried to enforce all the petty rules and regulations of the Employment Service, but she was naturally ineffective.

Whenever anyone disagreed with her, her hands began to fondle each other, her mouth twitched and her blue eyes glazed. She earned the contempt of those who worked under her—except a few who took pity and pretended indifference. I never heard her utter a Spanish word, and that, along with her pale complexion, blond hair, and blue eyes, led me to assume that she was not Hispanic until Lydia informed me otherwise.

"You're kidding me, right?"

"Would I kid you?"

"Yes, you would."

"Well, you're right; I would, but not about this."

"So what's the matter with you women? You don't like Spanish surnames?"

"Schmidt is my paternal name. That's beyond my control. Green is her married name."

"So what's her real name?"

"It's a secret. I can't tell you."

"Oh, come on."

"Maybe I'll tell you someday if you're nice to me."

Green's incompetence, more relevant than her paternal name, resulted in her being ignored about work matters as well as social ones—something she took to heart, having no inkling as to the cause of her unpopularity. She was not, after all, a mean person, but she failed to recognize her own ineptitude. When the office ran out of paper because she had forgotten to sign the request, she didn't see the inconvenience as any reflection on her performance.

She didn't know how to socialize with the people under her supervision though she showed some good intention. She surprised everyone one day by buying a cake for the staff. Everyone wondered what special occasion had prompted her, until she made a little speech to declare the cake a small treat meant as thanks for the fine work being done. Seeing her discomfort, we each politely took a bite of cake.

To compensate for her ineptitude, Mrs. Green needed someone to assist her, someone she could trust, someone with whom she saw eye to eye. Jay Finney was the only available candidate who met those requirements. Disliked as much as Mrs. Green, the two were a pair.

In the hierarchy of the Employment Service, a counselor ranks above an interviewer although they perform the same tasks. Finney, one of two counselors in the unit, did even less. He, being the senior counselor, stopped dealing with the public after his desk was moved next to Mrs. Green's. In his new capacity, he sat hunched over, pen in hand, furiously wasting ink on government stationery. No one ever read what he wrote.

Occasionally, he passed a note to an interviewer indicating some minor transgression of service regulations. No one on the staff felt any compunction when tearing up the note in his face. His questionable promotion moved him from being considered foolish to being judged obnoxious. The scorn of his fellow workers, however, he bore with more equanimity than his fear of the public. He was glad to escape the need to interview anyone, a task at which he had been a constant failure.

In interviewing, he had no style whatsoever. He was apt to conduct a whole interview without looking at the applicant and conclude, still hunched over filling in the blanks in the application, the fingers of his left hand tapping on the desk, "There's nothing we can do for you right now, and it seems to me that it behooves you to learn English before you come back."

The applicant, hardly understanding, caught the words "nothing now." The rest were a mystery to her. She came hoping to find a job as a floor girl in some factory, but after waiting for two hours, there was nothing. She sat very still waiting to be told what she must do next.

Finney looked up from his writing and managed enough courage to lean back in the swivel chair and repeat: "I really think it *behooves* you to make an effort to learn English." The words emerged with more force than he intended.

"*Jes, lern Ingles,*" the applicant said. The ramifications of *behooves* were lost on her but not on the other interviewers who were listening.

Later, at lunchtime, we mimicked the counselor. "It *behooves* you. . .," someone says, nose sticking up in the air. Everyone laughs.

I shared an office with Antonio Rivera. He was only twenty-one, the youngest interviewer on the staff. Despite his youth, he already owned a house and a big car, and had a wife to whom, faithful to his concept of manhood, he was unfaithful. His infidelities something to brag about to his colleagues of either sex, everyone knew about his cheating—his young wife the only one he didn't tell. He ran around with as many women as possible believing infidelity to be a man's prerogative. No one could deny his manhood, *macho completo*.

Everyone in the office, inclined to be interested in everyone else's personal life, enjoyed the ongoing news of Antonio's extramarital escapades. His stories generated sympathy for his wife, Mariana, who was only seventeen. He introduced her to us, and we found her charming and looked forward to her growing up to give Antonio the thrashing he deserved.

"It's better to marry a young woman," Antonio tried to explain. "That way you can mold her as a wife. If you marry someone older, that's too hard to do."

"Yeah, and who's molding you?" the question typically came from the women in the office.

Antonio didn't let his young wife go out to work. She stayed home and kept house even though they still had no children.

"She'll have plenty to do when the children come," Antonio said.

"Any time soon?" Lydia Sotomajor asked. She was thirty-one and still single. Everyone suspected that she was seeing a married man.

"Not yet, but soon," Antonio answered.

"Will you stop fooling around when you have children?" she continued to needle him.

Antonio took it in stride. Paradoxically, he felt compelled to warn me of the dangers of such activity.

"You're going to get shot," Antonio said to me.

"I didn't do anything," I protested.

"You don't have to do anything," Antonio argued. "All you have to do is to seem like you're doing something."

During our lunch hour, he had seen me walking, arm in arm with the new receptionist. We had gone around the corner to a sandwich place and then to her apartment down the block to pick up a record player for the office party to take place that afternoon.

"The record player was too heavy for her to carry," I explained.

"What record player?"

"Oh, it turned out to be missing."

And in fact, once in the apartment Margarita remembered that a cousin had borrowed the machine, impossible to retrieve it that afternoon. When I explained, Antonio cocked his head, and his eyes widened knowingly. A smile escaped the mesh of his moustache and goatee. Come, come, I'm a man. I know about these things.

That afternoon, the festivity proceeded without the record player.

"Are you married?" Margarita asked me.

"No, but someone lives with me."

"Then you're married," she assured me.

"Don't let it bother you," I quipped.

"Oh, I won't. I'm married too, and I have a baby."

"And you're so young!"

"I'm twenty."

"You look younger."

Nibbling on Colonel Sanders' chicken legs and potato salad, Margarita and I sat by the open door. People who walked into the room to get their helping, glancing in our direction, quickly looked away.

"Tch, tch, what are you doing behind the door?"

We both looked up at a short dark figure with a protruding belly, Anna, in whose honor the party was being held. She was six months pregnant and leaving for that reason, Margarita taking her place as receptionist.

"Leave married women alone, Mario. It's trouble," Anna smiled. Her little brown eyes seemed to want to pop out of her head. "Margarita, you have to watch out for Mario. He used to flirt with me all the time, but he knows my husband comes to pick me up from work every day."

Margarita continued nibbling away, a smudge of chicken grease on her face, the very picture of innocence.

"Mario is a good boy," she finally said.

"I'm sure he's good," Anna turned her puffy face to look straight at me.

"Why are you sure?" I asked. "You have no idea whether I'm good or not."

"Don't get fresh with me," she replied affecting haughtiness.

The well-spiked punch made Anna happy and pleasant. Like everyone else, I was a little afraid of her. She was known for a ferocious temper surprising to behold in such a physically small person. In the crowded waiting room, when after hours of fruitless waiting applicants became unruly, her temper came in handy. A mouse acting as a lion tamer, she carried it off very well. I saw her break down only once. Insulted by a man who claimed that unfairly others were being interviewed before him, she had burst into tears. Margarita had yet to face the waiting room crowd by herself. Everyone expected her to have less control than Anna. At the moment, Anna's cheerful mood put me at ease.

"Have some punch," Anna said, extending the paper cut toward Margarita.

"I can't drink. I get dizzy."

"It's not very strong."

"I'll get you some," I said. I rushed to the punch bowl and brought back two cups of the concoction, one for Margarita.

She shook her head. "No, please," she said, "unless you want to carry me home."

I emptied my cup and hers too.

2

At the end of the day, Margarita, Antonio, and I left the third-floor office together. Margarita on my arm, we took the stairs, faster to walk down than to take the erratic elevator. As we approached the street door, Antonio pulled me back to let Margarita exit ahead of us. She reluctantly released my arm.

"Are you still protecting my life?"

"Somebody has to," Antonio answered. "You don't know who might be on the other side of that door."

We proceeded through the door to see three men on the stoop, two in suits. The third, in shirtsleeves, short, large belly, no neck, had he been wearing a red robe rather than blue sharkskin pants and a white shirt open at the collar, he would have been a ringer for the Little King. Antonio nodded in the direction of the three. The belly-man acknowledged the greeting. To me they were strangers. I glanced at them, then looked toward Margarita already half way up the block. Her dress clung attractively to her hips. I had the desire to follow her, but I diverted my gaze and descended to the sidewalk. Leaning against a car, several young men chatted, the one wearing a plaid hat, Anna's husband.

"He does pick her up every day."

"He certainly does."

"Doesn't he work?"

"He has to. He's on parole. I think he's a welder's apprentice in a scrap iron place on Bruckner Boulevard."

"He must get out by four-thirty to make it here by five."

"There wasn't enough to drink at this party. Let's go over to Ralph's," Antonio suggested.

"All right, just a little while," I said looking at my watch.

"You know the fat man was Perez, top guy running the center and in control of the money coming in from Washington," Antonio said. "The War on Poverty is in high gear. It's good to let him notice us."

"And you think we're part of the poor," I said.

"That's not the point; is it, now?"

I smirked and let the matter drop. We proceeded to Ralph's Bar; a gentler sort tended to hang out there. We sometimes went for lunch to Harry's Pub farther away, a white place; it had good sandwiches. At Ralph's, I asked for a daiquiri. The bartender said he didn't know how to make it. He didn't know how to make a whisky sour either. I had a scotch and soda. I had two before Antonio had finished his one, the reverse of the usual. After a while, we moved to a booth. Ralph, the owner, an Irishman, sat in a booth at the rear, a German shepherd at his feet. The bartender was black, and so was everybody else in the bar except Antonio and me, and of course, Ralph.

"You're drinking hard," Antonio said.

"Pacifying the demons."

"You're a fuck'n intellectual," Antonio said. "What demons?"

"You know what kind of women I hang out with?"

"All women are demons."

"That's not what I said, and that's not what I mean."

"In that case, I apologize for jumping to the right conclusion. Proceed with your dissertation."

"Can you believe that I never had a Puerto Rican girlfriend?"

Of course, I remembered my cousin Lilian. We had loved each other when we were children. In Puerto Rico, our parents had put us in the crib together and chuckled at the sight of us lying next to each other.

As we grew up, we romped the countryside. Once, caught in an eddy in the river, close to the wooden bridge Grandfather had built, I struggled as Lilian shouted for the others to come save me. My cousins made a human to chain to reach out and pull me in.

She and I bathed together, and when we were a little older, and our families came to live in New York, we hung out and often went to the movies together. I expected that closeness to last forever, but when we became teenagers, the unexpected wall that suddenly appeared shocked me.

"Never?"

I shook my head.

"Oh, well, you don't know what you're missing."

"Your sarcasm I don't need! Are you going to listen?"

112

"I'm listening."

"Well, now there's Margarita. . ."

"Forget about Margarita. She's trouble. She's married. She has a kid. Besides all that, she's too young."

"Twenty is not too young."

"She's seventeen. I asked Myra; she takes care of the personnel files."

"Isn't your wife just seventeen? And why were you asking about Margarita's age?"

"I was curious, just curious. Forget about her. I'll fix you up with somebody else."

"No, Margarita is just right."

"Margarita is all wrong. Her husband is an addict. People like that can get desperate. I don't want to see you bleeding in the street."

"You're paranoid. That's what you are." I emptied another glass.

"Don't you ever read the paper? In New York, Puerto Ricans are always shooting other Puerto Ricans. It's an ethnic trait brought out by the climate—like asthma."

"Have we ever shot anybody?"

"We're different, you and I."

"What's that supposed to mean?"

"Nothing, nothing, let's get out of here; you're getting drunk."

I had difficulty keeping my balance as I eased my way out of the booth. I made an extraordinary effort to walk a straight line to the door but, once there, I couldn't figure out whether the door had to be pushed or pulled in order to get it to comply. A most stubborn door! An obstinate door! But it couldn't resist the might of two.

3

On Friday, just before quitting time, Antonio said to me, "I have a whole bottle of scotch. Come help me drink it."

"You have your wife to drink with," I replied.

"Mariana doesn't drink. She's involved with Jehovah's Witnesses, and now she's even trying to get me to stop drinking."

"It must be an epidemic. Margarita is on some kind of religious kick too. Look what she slipped into my pocket." I pulled out a palm-size booklet with a green cover. *Gospel of St. John* the title read.

"Did she tell you her scheme?" Antonio asked me. "She wants to dedicate her life to helping drug addicts. As if she hasn't done that already. I told her the sensible thing to do is to throw that husband of hers out on the street."

"We're all afraid to be alone."

"He takes her money. She wants to find a job that pays more, so she'll have enough to support his habit and the household too."

We drove under the El along Westchester Avenue. The streets of my childhood familiar although decay had set in, abandoned buildings loomed around us. When I was a boy, the decay had yet to become obvious, though in the street, I routinely rubbed elbows with gang members.

"See that grocery store coming up," Antonio said. "My mother used to own it."

"Pretty big store."

"Good business! Used to clear over fifteen hundred on a Saturday. But it's too much for a woman to run by herself, especially now with the neighborhood the way it is. We never did have a robbery back then. People complain about the cops, but they're good for business. In the wintertime, they'd come and warm themselves in the back room—better than walking the beat. In the summer, they'd play cards back there. Everybody knew where they hung out, so nobody would try to stick up the place, never sure whether there wouldn't be a cop in the back."

"One man's gain is the loss of another."

"You're an intellectual," Antonio said, "a fuck'n intellectual."

"My father washed dishes when we first came to New York. Seven of us lived in a three-room apartment right near here, on Rogers Place. Don Justino, the grocer across the street, owned a brick house with a row of garages in the back. He made money from the store and the garages. He kept a vicious dog in the store for protection. That dog was really something—always muzzled and chained to the butcher block.

"He had a son, Tony, who had a reputation for being somewhat of a rake. I remember his hair, very black and shiny—a great deal of hair lotion. One time, Tony got too close to the dog. It lunged at him, and he grabbed a cleaver from the meat counter and went for the animal. His father rushed the dog outside. Tony followed brandishing the cleaver. People in the street held him back while the old man tried to control the dog. A great show, father and son cursing at each other, the dog growling, straining at the harness and trying to leap at Tony. All the windows on the block crowded with people watching the spectacle.

"Don Justino considered that dog more valuable than his son. From then on, Tony stayed away from the store. A couple of months later the dog attacked Don Justino, chewed away part of his left forearm and made a gash in his face. Still he kept the dog."

"Dogs like that are more trouble than they're worth."

"Kept him from being robbed."

"Could have killed him."

"A man has to risk something to protect his property."

"Not his life. You don't risk your life for money."

"For what then?"

Neither of us knew the answer to that.

Antonio made an unexpected turn into a seemingly uninhabited street, the windows of many of the buildings covered with tin, others with only boards. Two junked cars parked on opposite curbs looked like the skeletons of prehistoric beasts picked clean by vultures and jackals. I gazed through the windshield searching for a sign of life.

"I just want to show you the worst block in the Bronx," Antonio said. "You park your car on this block, and in five minutes it looks like those other two. Invisible creatures come out of those buildings and in no time devour all the soft parts. Only the steel bones are left. Makes you wonder what lives there."

We sped north on the Bruckner Expressway, leaving the slum behind. Five-story apartment buildings gave way to a landscape of two-family houses—each one looking exactly like the one next to it and each side of the street a mirror image of the other. Here and there a high-rise broke the horizontal monotony only to substitute a vertical one.

At his place, all the furniture had the predictable look. Every room resembled a store window display, harsh and impersonal. I walked to the window and peered through the Venetian blind. The fantasy that in the house across the street my exact double did the same thing made me smile. This was not a living room but a copy of someone's ideal image of a living room.

"Let's go down to the basement. It's much nicer there," Antonio said. "I spend most of my time down there, or. . .," he added winking, "in the bedroom. I'm a bedroom/basement man, you might say."

In the basement, black light pulsated dots on the dark walls, and psychedelic posters further impaired concentration.

"This is my favorite," Antonio said pointing at a poster from which a bare-breasted young woman stared, glassy eyed but smiling, the field behind her filled with unnatural shapes. "Doesn't she remind you of Margarita?"

I shook my head, annoyed at the comparison.

"Look at the shape of the face framed by that long black hair. And the mouth! Just like Margarita's!"

I had no will to argue, the room filled with energy that somehow prevented me from directing my own. I made an effort to keep from dissolving—if I relaxed, my body might be absorbed by the decor of the room. I sipped the drink Antonio had prepared. "It's hard to drink in this room," I said, annoyed though I didn't exactly know why.

"What do you mean? It's perfect for drinking!" Antonio protested. He paused and dropped the self-assured attitude he took on at work. On his own ground, he became vulnerable. "I don't keep anything in the house that Mariana disapproves of. One has to make some concessions."

"I thought you were out to educate her," I said, immediately sorry to have lost control of my tongue. I liked Antonio, a young copy of the older Ortegas, what they all had expected me to become.

He ignored my comment and continued, "We can go to my cousin Shorty's, after dinner. I want you to see his place—really freaky—and he always has grass."

4

A few days later, Antonio returned to the old topic of protecting me. "I think you have to watch your step," he said.

"I'm clean," I retorted.

"You're an amateur at this kind of thing," he continued.

I didn't take him seriously. After all, I hadn't done anything I considered wrong or even risky. He was exaggerating a trivial matter, flirting with the receptionist, to what it would be if he were the one playing with the young lady.

"I'm going to take you out to lunch," he said to me. "I know a great place, and I brought a bottle of great wine."

"It's not my birthday," I said. "What's the occasion?"

"Well, although you're older than me, there are some things I can teach you."

"I know how to drink wine," I said.

"Well, there are other things." He grinned to exhibit the *macho* attitude required when dealing with another man.

"We'll have to drive there," Antonio said.

So we drove up to Eastchester and pulled into a pizza place. I hadn't eaten pizza in many years. When I was a boy, the smell of the cheese had made me nauseous. I didn't yet know that in New York the cheese used for pizza had changed.

"Hey, you know I don't like pizza," I right away said.

"This is the best pizza place in the city. You'd never expect to find it up here in the Bronx, run by Puerto Ricans. Wonders never cease; you're going to have pizza, with wine of course."

"I'm telling you, the last time I had pizza I threw up."

Antonio ignored my reluctance and ordered a whole pizza. A little disturbing since even if out of politeness I ate one piece, he would still have to deal with the rest. I didn't want to encourage him. By my standards, he was already too heavy to eat more than necessary.

He kept talking while we waited for the pizza. "I don't blame you for running after Margarita, but with her you have to be careful."

He took the matter more to heart than anyone else, including Margarita who, from her post at the front desk, flirted with all the men who came by. "Everyone sees you flirting with her," he continued. "And everyone is talking about it. I understand your impulse to be out in the open. I don't keep secrets myself, but I'm careful who I mess with, if you know what I mean."

"No, I don't know what you mean."

"I mean you have to be careful about whose wife you're dealing with. He's a drug addict, right? You can't depend on someone like that to be rational. He's the kind of guy who would come after you with a gun."

"You know him?"

"Not really, but he's into drugs, right? That tells you everything. If he finds out about you and Margarita, he's going to come after you."

"There's nothing to find out," I insisted.

"Sure," Antonio said as he got up to fetch the pizza from the counter. He brought it to the table and went back for a couple of plastic cups for the wine.

"And how are we going to open this bottle?"

"*Voilà*," Antonio said pulling out his pocketknife that had a corkscrew. "I come prepared for all eventualities. You should do the same."

"I'll buy a Swiss Army knife on my way home," I said.

"I don't think that'll do any good against a gun," Antonio

said. "Really, I mean what I'm saying. You have to be careful with Margarita."

The slight pop of the cork announced the entrance of the wine. Methodically, Antonio unscrewed the cork from the corkscrew, folded the knife, and put it back in his pocket. "Now have some Italian wine," he said, "goes with pizza."

"Italian, wow," I exclaimed. "I thought you were bringing Puerto Rican wine."

"I have that too," he retorted, "for special occasions, speaking of which, I'm having a party in a couple of weeks.

"Can I bring Margarita?"

"Don't be funny; you know she's not your type."

I took a slice from the platter, and as I brought it up to my mouth, I closed my eyes. The old odor I had expected from the cheese absent, I bit into the slice to be overwhelmed by the spectacular taste.

5

When I arrived in the morning, some of the women were still chatting by the elevator. Rosie Rodriquez, secretary to Albert Tickney, one of the top guys in the community center, looked like she had been in a brawl the night before.

"What happened to your eye, Rosie?" Paula asked, though she had guessed before Rosie answered.

"What happened? He found out," Rosie said smiling.

"Who found out what?"

"Frankie found out about Julio."

"What are you going to tell your boss?" Margarita asked.

"He's cool," Rosie said. She had confidence in her charm.

"Put some makeup on it—it won't look so bad."

"Shit, if I touch it, I'll see stars. Best to leave it alone. I don't give a damn how it looks."

Luz walked in holding a large cup of coffee. She looked in the direction of the three young women to deliver the usual "good morning," but noticing Rosie's eye, she walked over instead of going straight to her office.

"*Que te paso en el ojo?*" She hardly spoke English.

"I bumped into a door, dear," Rosie said turning to go.

They didn't like Luz. They suspected her of being a spy for Perez. She was getting paid to fill the post of psychological tester for which she was unqualified. She had dropped out of the University of Puerto Rico, and she didn't know enough English to read the instructions on the test booklets.

"I guess she has domestic problems," I said after Rosie took the elevator up to Tickney's office on the fifth floor.

"She has bad luck with men," Paula said. "She's already a mother and a widow."

"Vietnam?"

"No, South Bronx."

"What?"

"Her husband OD'd. Now she plays with men who play rough."

"If you play with fire. . .," Margarita said.

"There's a saying about glass houses."

"Women are always talking," I interjected on my way to my desk.

I took off my jacket and hung it on the back of my chair. About to sit down, I noticed Mrs. Green peering at me from across the hall. I had overlooked signing the time sheet. I nodded a good morning to her. The workday yet to begin, I already longed to depart. I signed the time sheet and went back to my desk. Antonio shortly joined me.

"God damn, she always has to stand over that time sheet," Antonio said in a low voice. He too had arrived late.

"She wants everything regular, so she can clinch that promotion."

"What promotion?"

"To manager."

"She can't be manager. There's an agreement with the community center that the office manager has to be black."

"The Labor Department can't do that. It's illegal."

"Well, it's understood. A lot of things around here are understood.

120

At this center there are too many PRs at the top. They need a few blacks to make it look good."

"That's no concern of ours. We work for the federal government."

"Whether you work for Uncle Sam or not, you can stop a bullet as well as anybody."

"There you go again. Don't you ever have anything else on your mind?"

"I'm telling you, things are getting hot around here. I went to a meeting Saturday night. They were almost ready to shoot it out."

"Wherever *you* go, people want to shoot it out."

"You think I'm kidding? The community corporation wants to take control of the funds for this center. Perez wants to retain control himself. Man, it's millions they're fighting over."

"So why were you there?"

"It's smart to let yourself be seen at meetings—you're a concerned citizen—so when you need a favor these guys have to come through. They don't care about doing anything for the whole community, but they have to care about the people who show up at the meetings. That's their power base."

"Well, you learned your civics!"

"All you need is common sense. How do you think Luz got that job? She sits in that office the whole day doing nothing. Twice a week she administers that test for an hour. She gets paid more than us. Everyday for two months, she came here to pester Perez until she got the job."

"She must do more than administer tests."

"Okay, so she snoops around a little. Everybody knows it, so it doesn't do any harm."

"Maybe not," I said.

Antonio's desk looked like the wastepaper basket had been emptied on it. As he attempted to create some order, I leaned back in my chair to watch the futile process. Margarita came in wearing her hair long that day. I noted her well-shaped nose, delicate lips, and very dark eyes.

"There are people in the waiting room," she announced.

"We just came up. Give us a moment to breathe."

"You're all as lazy as Luz," Margarita said. "Did you notice how she's putting on weight around the middle?"

"This kind of work isn't good for weight watchers," I said.

"Only her belly is getting bigger. She says she's having gland trouble."

"She should see a doctor."

"I think the treatment might be expensive," Margarita continued maliciously.

"No kidding? In what sort of gland do you suppose the problem originated?" Antonio inquired while still trying to set his desk in order.

"The question is not what sort but whose."

Mrs. Green came to the door. She waited there for a moment to let her presence be noted. Pouting a little more and batting her eyelashes she said, "Let's not keep the public waiting."

No one moved. Mrs. Green waited another moment, batted her eyelashes again, then walked to the next room to deliver the same message.

"I'm ready," I said to Margarita. "Bring'm in."

Margarita, the first person encountering the clients, made a quick judgment as to which of the interviewers would be the best match for each person who came by her desk. Having made that determination, she dropped each application form in the appropriate assignment box.

She yelled out, "Rodriguez!" The volume startled both Antonio and me.

"You have no class," Antonio said.

"I don't tell you how to interview, so don't tell me how to do my job," she retorted.

Rodriguez, a short thin man who seemed nervous, appeared at the door. He looked at the mess on Antonio's desk then at the telephone books holding up one corner of it, but he didn't dare smile.

Margarita pointed to the chair by my desk, and Rodriguez sat down.

"Speak English?" I asked.

"No."

"Has trabajado anteriormente?" I continued. I was developing a difficulty rolling my R's.

He had worked on road construction in Puerto Rico. After the completion of the road, he had no job, so he migrated to New York. I shuffled some papers on my desk. I kept a very serious expression on my face as if performing an arduous task. I knew how many papers I would have to leaf through before I got to the right one. I could have picked it out right away, but I pretended I had a file full of possibilities. When I had it in my hand, I described the one job available at the moment that didn't require English—at an office furniture factory, a dollar eighty an hour, twenty cents over the minimum. The man said he would try it if there was nothing else. I wrote out the introductory card and handed it to him.

Margarita had brought an applicant over to Antonio's desk. "Do you have any place I can send a man who doesn't speak English?" he asked me.

"I'm sending this one to Comfort Steel," I said. "You can send him too. They always hire."

"What do they make?"

"Office furniture," I said rapping my knuckles on my desk.

"No!" Antonio exclaimed, leaning back and cocking his head.

"We got these at a big discount," I said.

Antonio filled out a card and handed it across the desk. Both his and my man left on their way to Comfort Steel.

6

At midday, Margarita came by. "Take a walk with me," she said. "It's lunchtime already."

I assumed she wanted to discuss something other than whether her shoes really matched her skirt. We stopped by the grocery store to buy a few items. "I have to be ready for when my son gets home," she said to me as she handed the money to the cashier. At the steps of her building, I offered to wait for her while she took the groceries upstairs.

"Come up," she said. "Don't be a ninny."

"I'm just trying look after your reputation," I said. "You do have neighbors."

"Well, here, carry my groceries. You'll have an excuse."

"I'm not the one who needs an excuse," I said.

And no one needing an excuse, I followed her up the steps to the rhythm of her swinging hips.

Henry Tilling

THE LABOR DEPARTMENT tried to assign as many Hispanic men as possible to the Bronx office, but the shortage of candidates resulted in Henry Tilling ending up in the Bronx along with Antonio and me as the male quota. Although everyone in the office considered Henry an odd fellow, we accepted him as one of the group. Seeing him as the Sad Sack, we constantly advised him on how to better his life.

He lived with Grace Hammett. Physically small, short dark hair, wore glasses that gave the impression of meekness, but that image dissolved after a few minutes of watching her manage Henry—a routine observed when we, along with our domestic partners, got together away from the office. She controlled every personal detail of his life. As if playing housekeeping with him as a full-size doll, she bought clothes for him on her own, choosing the style and the color without asking him. He never made a decision without consulting her, and she always had the final word. In any case, that's what we all thought based on his own description of his domestic life.

"And you let her do that to you?" Antonio repeatedly asked.

"What can I do? I've grown used to her."

"Don't you want to be a man?"

"What can I do?"

"Get another woman," Antonio's solution to every possible male problem.

One morning, as soon as he arrived at the office, Henry announced that he had moved out of his apartment leaving Grace behind, along with everything else except his clothes. He had packed a suitcase and moved in with a new girlfriend.

"What new girlfriend?"

"I just met her two weeks ago."

"Two weeks and she let you move in?"

"We're in love," he said.

Henry Tilling being the last person from whom anyone in the office expected a sudden move, this development excited everyone. Of course, after short reflection, the overlooked signs became obvious. He had been constantly telling us about his problems with Grace, and we had all, including the women, urged him to take action. Whether we expected him to do so is another matter, but now we all had an opinion on whether the event indicated a change in his personality.

"Well, we can't tell yet," I said.

"You're right," Lydia agreed.

"What are you talking about?" Antonio put in. "This is a big change."

"We haven't met the new woman. For all we know, she's just the old one with a different face."

That was the most likely possibility. When acquiring a new partner, the choosing of a person similar to the previous one was a common explanation for the phenomenon of multiple divorces. Henry's eagerness to introduce his new friend went along with everyone's desire to verify that he had made a good choice, so we arranged to all go out to dinner. We convened at the new couple's apartment, which had been solely hers until Henry moved in. Together they had painted and redecorated to show that they were both in a new place, physically and emotionally.

Henry's new girlfriend, Nancy Trevor, another of those young people coming to the city to launch their careers, had been an art major at some small midwestern college. Once in New York, she landed a job in an advertising agency, the starting salary unimpressive but in a position to learn the business, and now she had acquired a domestic partner to keep her from being lonely in the big city. As Henry's fellow workers, we were pleasantly surprised, though still somewhat puzzled, when we met the young woman. She bore no resemblance to her predecessor, physically or otherwise.

Nancy's poise and elegance contrasted with Henry's. The redoing of the apartment, we guessed, was the most obvious expression of the difference between them. The unusual exhibit of an artistic bent impressed us, the inner wall of the living room painted triangularly, the upper part in a pleasant mauve, a color none of us had ever seen in a domestic setting. Each of the apartment's four rooms had something unusual to express the new couple's character, except that no one could tell from where in Henry this taste had emerged.

We assumed that his input had been completely overshadowed by Nancy's. We suspected that she would use her talent to dominate him the way Grace had used her impulse to manage. In front of the group, however, Nancy seemed to be expecting the opposite from Henry. She deferred to him whenever possible and treated him as if he were demanding the traditional male prerogatives. No one else saw any change in his behavior, and we concluded that she had let her creative imagination distort her view of the man.

Back in the office on Monday, Henry's new relationship continued to be the topic of discussion.

"I guess he found the woman who lets him be a man," Lydia concluded.

"The question is: what does she get out of it?"

"Well, he's a nice guy."

"Let's hope that's enough," I commented, very much doubting that it would be.

Two weeks later at the office, Mr. Ramos, who had the semblance of an overstuffed rag doll—medium height, moustache, dusky complexion—appeared at the door. "You have any training programs for women?" he asked, his standard question. Standing behind him, a bleach blond—her mouth caked with red lipstick, her eyebrows plucked, brown lines drawn up into the temples, presumably where she wished her natural eyebrows had been—stuck her head into the office.

Mr. Ramos was attached to Manpower, the overall department in which the Employment Service functioned. In reality, the Employment Service, part of the U.S. Department of Labor, was independent from the rest of the center, but it served as the core and the only useful section. Everyone else, from the center director to the lowest clerk, engaged in tasks for which they had themselves created the need. Mr. Ramos had no obvious duties to occupy him. Nevertheless, he had an office with his name on the door and the title Coordinator of Client-Center Relations. His immediate superior, the director of the manpower division, who knew how to perpetually look busy, constantly exhorted him to do something but never specified the tasks. He didn't understand why Mr. Ramos lacked the good sense to keep busy. Mr. Ramos came across both extremely dense and absolutely sure that no matter how much he embarrassed the organization he wouldn't be fired.

The employment interviewers marked him as both incompetent and sure of his post and found those two conditions difficult to reconcile. If he were as stupid as he so often acted, how did he ingratiate himself sufficiently to obtain and retain a post that could easily be filled by anyone? His ineptitude was so blatant that a sanctioned excuse for retaining him had to be found. That resulted in the official explanation: that he had been one of the early fighters for Puerto Rican rights in New York, and now past his heyday, he was being rewarded for his pioneering work.

How much he fought for anyone's rights may be deduced from his comment that only lazy people who didn't want to work showed up at the Employment Service. According to him, jobs were so abundant one could just stumble into them. We interviewers arrived at the consensus that Ramos had a stranglehold on one of the directors on the board, possibly on Perez, the top man. But in that case, Mr. Ramos was a clever man indeed to manage staying alive.

"Henry takes care of training referrals," Antonio said to Mr. Ramos. "You know that."

"I don't like to deal with him. You know, he's not one of us. One of you fellows should do it," said Mr. Ramos, directing the remark at Antonio and me.

"No trouble with anyone, if you follow the proper procedure," I said to Mr. Ramos.

"We can't take people out of turn. You know there's a waiting list for training," Antonio added.

"In emergencies you have to make exceptions," Mr. Ramos rejoined.

"You have an emergency?"

"Yes, this young lady is an emergency," Mr. Ramos said turning to the blond who wasn't exactly young. Her already disfigured face became more so with expressions of disgust and impatience. Mr. Ramos had promised to get her into a training program, and she had not expected so much idle talk. She realized that he was stalling and not talking to anyone who could get her in.

"I should have set up a law practice and avoided all this," Mr. Ramos lamented.

"So, you're a lawyer," I said.

"Yes, I have a degree from a correspondence school, but only three states recognize it as valid."

"You should be working with the legal department," I said.

"New York is not one of the states that recognizes my degree," Mr. Ramos sadly answered. For a moment, he became someone other than the bungling bully, his little brown eyes seemingly looking away to one of the three states.

"Henry's office is down the hall. About training, you have to talk to him."

"Yes," he said, and turning about, he walked down the hallway followed by the blond.

"I have to see this," Antonio said getting up from his desk. "Henry found out about the little racket Mr. Ramos ran at the Manpower office on 149th Street. He got all these women into the training programs, and they kicked back part of their stipend. When they completed one training program, they went on to another. Some were in four or five of them, Mr. Ramos taking money from them all."

"You think Henry has enough balls to do anything about it?"

"That's what I want to see."

Antonio followed Ramos down the hall to the waiting room directly across from Henry's office. Under the pretext of discussing with Margarita, the receptionist, some matter about the applications, he waited to see what would happen. Mr. Ramos, however, had the good sense to close the door behind him once he had walked into Henry's office, leaving Antonio in the lurch, scarcely able to hear anything being said on the other side.

"Why don't you put your ear to the door?" Margarita smirked.

He thought that a good idea and did so, but he still couldn't clearly hear what Henry was saying. Except that in a few minutes, Henry's voice became louder, and Antonio didn't have to be that close to the door to hear, "Get out! Get out of here, right now!"

In a second, Mr. Ramos, his face as calm as when exiting a confessional, came out followed by the woman who had reached the conclusion that she had made the mistake of allying herself with a buffoon.

Walking back to his desk, Antonio said to me, "Oh, boy, maybe Henry's getting to be a man. That new woman of his may be doing the job."

"Maybe," I said. "We'll have to wait and see, won't we?"

The following week, when Henry arrived at the office on Monday morning, Lydia immediately noticed something drastically different. Having placed his usual cup of morning coffee on the right-hand corner of his desk, he accidentally knocked it over when she stopped by for the usual morning banter. Luckily for her, she stepped back quickly enough to avoid getting any stains on her clothes, and only paper on Henry's desk was damaged.

"Oh, God! Oh, God!" he said as if he had just ruined documents of national importance. Only statistics were forwarded to the central office at the end of the month, numbers very often creatively manufactured on the very day they were due, a fact at the moment obscured by his emotional reaction. His face had taken on a greenish hue, which Lydia first attributed to his fear of having incurred her wrath for possibly having damaged her clothes. She tried to assure him that everything was all right. "You missed me, tough guy, nothing to worry about," she said in her cheerful morning mood, a condition that usually dissipated as the day progressed.

"I don't know if I can make it through the day," he said, jumping up and visually scouring the neighboring desks for paper towels to clean the mess. He righted the paper cup, all the coffee gone, the lid having been discarded before he sat down.

True, the cup had been only half full when he knocked it over. For that at least, he had to be thankful, a fact which Lydia pointed out before telling him to go out to the front desk and get paper towels from Margarita, who, kind enough, tackled cleaning the whole mess without being asked. She had noticed Henry's discomfiture as he walked in that morning. Trying to figure out everyone's mood for the day had become part of her job.

"Oh, extra coffee," I said as I walked in. Both women gave me a look to let me know more was going on than was readily apparent. "Well, how was everybody's weekend?" I continued, not bothering to figure out what they were trying to tell me and attributing Henry's discomfort to the coffee spill.

"I see you ladies can't get away from housework," Antonio remarked as he walked in right after me. Lydia had decided to help Margarita clean up, mostly because the faster they got rid of the coffee mess the quicker they might get Henry to explain his mood. If physically ill, he should go home and spare everyone else from catching whatever he had.

"I'm falling apart," Henry said, looking past the women to where Antonio and I were sitting.

"It's only coffee," Antonio said, "and you have a clean-up crew."

"Nancy threw me out," Henry gasped as if his head had just emerged from a swimming pool after having dived much deeper than he had intended.

His announcement, followed by a silence no one wanted to take responsibility for breaking, failed to provide sufficient comfort to the suffering Henry.

"What am I to do?" he asked, transforming the wall into an oracle that would reveal to him the ideal path.

"Do you have a place to stay?" Lydia inquired.

"Just a room in a boardinghouse."

"She'll take you back. Just be patient and apologize for whatever you did."

"It wasn't like that," he said with almost a sob.

No one mentioned the obvious path he should take, the one that would lead him straight back to Grace Hammett. No one uttered the words, but he read our faces. Pride, however, kept him from immediately accepting that solution.

"Nancy said she woke up. She didn't know what she was thinking when she let me move in with her."

"What are you worried about?" Antonio said. "A woman is like a bus. If you miss one, there'll be another one along in five minutes."

"Listen, Antonio," Lydia chimed in, "I think we can do without your outdated attitude right now."

"Hey, it works for me," Antonio retorted.

"Grace won't take me back. I just know she won't," Henry continued.

"She will," Antonio assured him. "She knows she had a good thing with you."

"You think she will?"

"Sure, she will."

"I don't know how I'm going to get through the day."

"Go home," Lydia urged.

"Yeah, go home," Antonio echoed. "Mario, don't you think he should go home?"

"Maybe it's better to be here with us under the circumstances," I said.

Henry sat at his desk for half an hour, and suddenly, without saying good-bye to anyone, he left.

He didn't return. He had a nervous breakdown and spent some time at a sanitarium.

Neighbors

CHUCK WALKED IN without knocking. When home, I often didn't bother to lock the door, an unusual practice in New York except on Renwick Street, an unusual place.

The whole street extended for only one block, with only two residential buildings, one at each end. During the workday the street bustled with truck drivers and other blue-collar workers, laborers who provided the street with a hometown feel. Moreover, the police exhibited a strong interest in the neighborhood. Their constantly visible nightly patrols functioned as private security for the warehouses, the neighborhood residents fortuitous beneficiaries.

"Shit, she left me," Chuck said.

"Who?" I asked, looking up from the frying pan where two slices of Spam absorbed my attention.

"Elizabeth walked out on me," he said.

Having gotten used to Chuck not looking for much response when he spoke, I kept my attention on the frying pan. Elizabeth, a tall thin woman who wore jingle bells on her wrists and ankles, had been living with him for two months.

"Sorry to hear that," I said after I concluded that the Spam indeed needed a few more minutes of medium flame. Jokingly I continued, "But you know, women come and go. You can just saunter over to Washington Square and pick one up."

A moment of silence, then, "Fuck it, man, you're right," Chuck said, and he sprung to his feet from his seat on the windowsill and walked out without another word, presumably on his way to Washington Square.

A few weeks later he dropped by again. This time he knocked on the door before entering. "Take a look at this," he said, handing me a photograph of a nude young woman obviously staged to avoid the label of pornography.

"A work of art," I said.

"A response to my ad in the *San Francisco Chronicle*. I got the idea while walking around Washington Square: *Young woman wanted, Summer in New York, Rent free, Send photograph.*"

"And you got a response?"

"I got ten responses. This is the best one. The only full photograph too. What do you think?"

"Go for it."

So before the end of June, Hillary arrived from San Francisco fully clothed, even more attractive in person than in the photograph.

2

Robert, my neighbor down the hall, an installer for Bell Telephone, usually got home about six o'clock in the evening, his work belt hanging with equipment that proclaimed his occupation.

"Hey, Mario," he said standing at the door.

I looked up from the frozen dinner that was failing its test, my mother's cooking the standard of comparison.

"A box of this stuff just fell off a truck down the street," Robert said. "It drove off, so I retrieved it. Too much for me, so these are for you." He handed me three dozen eggs.

"You giving them away?"

"Sure, what am I going to do with a whole case?"

I put the eggs in the refrigerator. They dominated my diet for a week.

3

I searched in vain for the can opener to tackle the lid on the Campbell's soup can. "Shit," I said and proceeded down the hall to Robert's door. I knocked several times and getting no answer, pushed the door open and stuck my head in. I spied a needle and syringe lying on the table. Sitting in a chair by his kitchen table, Robert, his arm still bound, had just injected himself. "You got my can opener?" I inquired but got no response. "You're out of it," I murmured and walked into the kitchen to search for the can opener.

I glanced at several drawings on the wall in the next room. Robert's artwork, good pen and ink, what the hell did he need to shoot up for? I shifted my focus back to the can opener. Ah, there it was. "Hey, Robert, don't keep taking my can opener without asking. What if you weren't home and the door was locked? I'd be up the creek without a can opener, right? Just ask for the damn thing, so I'd know where to look for it." Of course, I knew where to look for it. I had gone looking for it, and I had found it. So why get upset? The can opener missing, a minor inconvenience; however, the electric fuses were a different matter altogether. The fuse box for my apartment out in the hallway, several times the fuses had been stolen. Anyone may have taken them, but of course, Robert was the usual suspect.

"Hey, Robert, can you hear me?"

Robert nodded his head but said nothing.

"Shit, you're somewhere else," I said and, can opener in hand, I went back to my Campbell's soup.

4

"Hi, I'm Suzie," a young Asian woman announced from the door. "I'm a friend of Robert's, down the hall. You know who I mean?"

"Sure, I know Robert," I said. I had seen Suzie enter the building several times, but we had not been introduced, and this was the first time we spoke. Standing at the door, she looked sick, and I suspected the reason.

"You haven't got any, have you?"

"Nah, I don't," I said. "You don't look well. You want to sit down?"

The young woman walked into the kitchen and sat at the table. I wondered what I could do for her. Then I wondered why I had invited her in. Someone in her state would be nothing but trouble. Still, she didn't look well.

"You want some tea?" I asked.

"Sure, if you have honey to put in it," she said.

I reached for the jar of honey in the cabinet above the stove, and I placed it on the table.

"Shit, that's something. You're amazing; I'm astounded," she said. "Most people don't keep honey."

"Is that so?" I inquired, deciding not to tell her that buying the honey had not been my idea but Isabel's, my partner who had taken off for San Francisco several weeks before. I proceeded to brew two cups of tea. She stirred three spoons of honey into hers and sipped. The cup still half full, Suzie's complexion turned green.

"Really, I don't feel well," she repeated.

"You should go home and lie down," I said.

"I don't want to be alone," she retorted.

"You can lie down in my bed," I said immediately wondering why I had said that. She was just trouble.

"All right," she said. Walking into the bedroom and crawling under the bedcover, she kept shivering. "I'm too cold," she said, her teeth clanking. "Hold me."

I lay down next to her under the covers, held her, but she kept shivering. I looked into her eyes and saw nothing. Only her body lay next to me, nothing else. In a while, she stopped shivering.

"I'm all right now," she said and got up. "Thanks for the tea."

Slowly, in a daze, she walked to the door. Just as she was about to put her hand on the doorknob, the door opened to reveal Chuck. He moved out of the way to let her pass, and I kept my eye on her as she moved down the hallway to Robert's place.

"She's no good," Chuck said to me. "I'd stay away from her if I were you."

"She's sick," I said.

"She's a druggie," Chuck said.

I stared at Chuck trying to figure out whether he excluded himself from that category.

"Yeah," I said.

"Hey, Hillary got a job as a cashier at Pioneer," he informed me then swerved and left.

"Well, good for her," I said, Chuck already by the steps.

I turned back into the kitchen and gazed at the table where the honey jar had been. "Shit, it's gone," I said to myself.

5

Larry Stuart had the apartment across from mine. Occasionally, we ran into each other out in the hallway. We said hello but nothing else. Larry always dressed impeccably, every strand of hair in place, his shoulders retrieved slightly beyond the normal.

"He's a bartender at Smokey's," Chuck informed me one time when, from my window, we saw Larry turn the corner on Spring Street.

"That's a gay bar," I said.

"Need I say more?" Chuck asked before making his exit.

Arriving home one day, I found a young woman and a child knocking on Larry's door and getting no response.

"I guess he's not home yet," I said to her.

Her dark eyes verged on tears, her face puffy as well as the rest of her body. She suddenly smiled conveying amiability as well as her willingness to accept help. The child retreated behind the young woman's skirt and intermittently peered out at me.

"You can come in here and wait if you want," I said.

"You don't mind?"

"Not at all, come in and sit down."

The young woman stepped in and sat down at the table. She picked up the little girl and sat her on her lap. "This is Cathy," she said. "I brought her down to visit her father."

"Her father?"

"Larry's her father," the young woman declared.

I silently mulled that over, life always interesting as well as complicated.

"I've been trying to persuade him, on the phone, to return home, but he refuses. I thought maybe if I brought Cathy down to see him, he'd realize she needs him."

In a while, we heard someone out in the hallway. I opened the door. On seeing the little girl beside her mother, Larry's expression of surprise transformed to one of consternation. He promptly recovered and opened his door to usher in his visitors. Looking at me, he flashed a smile and quickly shut the door in the vain hope, I assumed, that nothing else would be disclosed. In a while, the voices across the hall grew louder, the talk transforming into an argument. Finally, the young woman broke down, and all I heard was her sobbing.

6

Pushing the shopping cart through the aisles at Pioneer Supermarket, I attempted to get my shopping done as quickly as possible. A can of coffee, a two-pound box of sugar, a container of milk, two cans of Campbell's vegetable soup, I went by the honey but decided to forget about it and headed for the checkout. I unloaded my shopping cart before I noticed Hillary with a wide smile at the register.

"Hi, there," she said.

"Enjoying working?" I facetiously asked.

"Hey, it's simple enough," she said as she rang up my items.

She passed me the receipt showing what I owed. I looked at her, and she flashed her wide grin. I pulled change from the pocket of my dungarees to hand her thirty-six cents.

"Well, see you around," I said, and I walked out to Sixth Avenue heading down to Renwick Street.

Yesterday

*W*E WERE STILL in high school when my friend Martin first pointed Isabel out to me. She had impressed him with some witty answers to a questionnaire about the cafeteria, or so he said, when he drew my attention to her as we sat on a bench near the Metropolitan Museum. The summer mood by Central Park cool, pleasant, and soothing, Isabel's look melded into the ensemble of obvious wealth across the street and the green environment of the park. A tall slender girl next to a curly-haired young man sporting a camera on a shoulder strap failed to impress me. I noted her style and took her elegant simplicity as an affectation.

"Let's go say hello," Martin suggested.

"Let's not bother them," I said.

Perhaps jealous of the young man with the camera, I longed to escape. I didn't know this girl, and at the moment, I didn't see in her anything special, other than she and her friend fit into the surroundings in a way that I didn't.

"Maybe you're right. No sense in barging in," Martin said. "Still, I think she's special."

That was my first notice of her the year before I entered college. Two years later I ran into her again, and I realized that Martin had been right. In search of my French class the first day of my sophomore year, I went to the assigned room at the wrong time. Isabel's being the only familiar face there, I sat next to her. In the course of our conversation, she mirthfully pointed out my error. Flustered, I excused myself, and plagued by the thought that she must think me an idiot, I sprinted out of the room.

We soon met again, and I found myself easily talking to her, but she remained distant. Even on her off days, when she walked from one class to another sleeping on her feet, slumbered through calculus and cut history, even then, she seemed extraordinary. After Emerson and His Contemporaries, we walked to the student center, I trying to persuade her to sit with me in the cafeteria, she invariably refusing. We would part, she to the snack bar where the more conservative set hung out and I to the cafeteria to mingle with the freaks, the dope fiends, the radical intellectuals who, in their heads, were all writing sequels to *Finnegan's Wake*.

While sitting in the library one winter afternoon attempting to wring some meaning from the volume before me, occasionally I looked up to observe through the tinted glass window the sun hovering over the trees. The warm rays massaged my forehead urging me to drowse. I shook myself and tried to focus on the page. At one of those moments, I looked up to see Isabel enveloped by the sunlight—in a simple dress, high heels, her hair tied back in a twist—the image imprinted in my memory forever.

2

After graduation, I didn't see Isabel anymore, though I had her phone number in my little book. She had given me the number when her father was interested in selling his car. Just by chance another acquaintance of mine was looking to buy, so Isabel gave me the number to pass on to him. Never did I dial it myself until Martin, on his return from his training stint in the National Guard, convinced me to contact her in order to facilitate his approach. I thought the idea absurd and urged him to do his own phoning. He argued that she wouldn't remember him, that he would stand a better chance if I reintroduced them. Reluctantly, I agreed to go along with his scheme.

I called. There was a silence at the other end. "You remember me?" I asked feeling like a fool for having let Martin talk me into such a stupid stunt.

"Yes, of course," Isabel said. "It's just that hearing from you is so unexpected."

"Yeah, it's been a long time."

"Yes, but I'm very glad to hear your voice."

"Maybe we can get together sometime," I continued.

"Yes," she said, and we arranged to meet Saturday afternoon.

As she sat on the edge of the fountain in Washington Square on that gray day, she looked sad and worn out. Still, her magic persisted. Through lunch at a little restaurant on Waverly Place we brought each other up to date.

"I have to get myself together," she said. "I have to get my life going. It's been difficult for me to do anything. I didn't do much in school, but at least I went there every day. It was something, not much, but something nevertheless. I hated to be there. I wanted to go to some other school, but my father wouldn't pay."

Over her shoulder, I looked into the street through the open door of the restaurant. I wouldn't have anything different. The tourists, the street vendors, the hustlers, the shops, everything that moved or stood still in the Village had the quality of paper cutouts among which we moved.

"I wouldn't have minded had we been poor," she continued wearily smiling, her voice receding into a dark distance to become hardly audible.

When we left the restaurant, we got caught in a downpour. She suggested we take shelter at my place, but first we stopped at a hobby store on Eighth Street to buy a chess set.

"Oh dear, you're soaked," the shopkeeper said. She took us into the back and gave us paper towels, little use against so much water. The situation became humorous. Everyone happy, Isabel and I split the cost of the chess set, two dollars for the pieces and two dollars for the board, and out we went, back into the rain to my place. I rigged a clothesline in the kitchen, and she wore my bathrobe while her clothes hung to dry. Sitting cross-legged on the bed, we played chess until the rain stopped.

"You remember Martin?"

"Who's Martin?"

"He went to high school with us. Don't you remember? He interviewed you once when he was taking a survey about the cafeteria? You impressed him with your answers."

"I don't remember," she said.

"Let's go visit him."

"Okay, if you want."

We went over to Martin's place, and she was extremely amused by it all. Martin had adopted a Spartan style. He had almost no furniture. The front room contained only his bed. It was the biggest room in the place. He explained that he would rather sleep there than in the small room in the back, which at the moment contained only a small table and two chairs. All the cabinets in his tiny kitchen were filled with cans of Campbell's soup. Isabel couldn't contain her mirth when he opened the refrigerator to reveal one container of milk, some halvah, and a package of kosher hotdogs.

We went out to Schurz Park and stumbled on a festivity under way on the tennis court, the nets having been removed for the evening. Isabel suggested that we try crashing, an idea that appealed to Martin as a way of impressing her.

"This is Gracie Mansion, there'll be guards at the gate," I pointed out, the last thing I wanted at the moment, an incident to mar what had so far been a pleasant day.

"How do you know it's the mayor's party?"

"Who else has parties in Schurz Park?"

"Maybe it's a public event."

"Anyway, we're not dressed for it."

"It doesn't seem to be a formal affair. Let me check," Martin said.

He headed for the gate. His routine consisted of always proceeding until someone got wise to him. On one occasion, we had employed the method to penetrate the basement of the Metropolitan Museum of Art, and after having walked about perusing the art in storage, we had simply walked out through the employee exit. I recognized the obvious value of the technique; nevertheless, I felt uncomfortable using it. Besides, it seemed to me a style more suited to the Marx Brothers.

"It's all right! Come on!" Martin shouted from the gate.

I hesitantly walked by the guard who didn't seem to care who attended the festivity.

"I told him we were friends of Mike Zukowsky," Martin said.

"Who's he?"

"Nobody," Martin answered. "I made up the name."

"I suspect he's letting everybody in," I said.

A band played on one side of the enclosure. Some people danced, but most just stood about in small groups talking and sipping drinks.

"What do you think is going on here?"

"Obviously a party."

We stood watching at the edge of the dancing area. The crowd consisted mostly of people older than us, some in evening attire but the greater number more casual.

"Let's ask somebody what the occasion is."

"There's nothing here for us," I said. "Let's leave."

"Don't be in such a hurry. Now that we're here, let's mingle."

A young man, in a sport jacket and tie, hair shorter than considered fashionable at the time, approached Isabel for a dance. She declined. The young man tried to persuade her. Every minute grew more uncomfortable, a quiet walk in the park all I had expected.

"No, I don't dance," Isabel insisted. The young man retreated sporting an expression of disbelief.

"There's someone I know," Isabel exclaimed gazing through the crowd, her face becoming totally animated in a way I had not seen all day.

She pointed out a young man, medium height and stocky, dressed informally in a sweater rather than a jacket. His features less than fine but passable enough, on that evidence alone he would have been suspected of unshakable integrity, but there lurked something more, something usually reserved for a politician. His face, a trick picture, revealed one image at first sight and a different one a second later— the effect, a constant shifting, ruthlessness radiating through a mask of casualness.

Noticing Isabel, he walked toward her with the slow but deliberate step of a man who believes in his own importance. In a burst of energy, she greeted him, and I was reminded of a flock of birds suddenly taking flight. She introduced him as Norman and quickly rattled off all the polite questions as to the health of his family. They moved off speaking of people and events unfamiliar to Martin and me, the two of us left to shift for ourselves.

Isabel soon returned in a more buoyant mood. "He's Skip's brother. Skip is my sister's boyfriend. And do you know what this party is for? A movie company that just finished filming in New York. Norman is covering the event for the *New Yorker*. He writes a movie column."

"Ah, a critic," I said.

"Well, he's not just a critic. He's written two books on Indochina."

The door had again opened to reveal a glimpse of another world. I didn't immediately understand what Isabel saw in Norman, but I accurately deduced that scholarly work was not her criterion. She had not read Norman's two books nor expected anyone else to have done so. His value stemmed from moving in her sister's circle.

"He'll probably be an ambassador someday," she said.

The prospect of Norman's ambassadorship did nothing to improve my mood. As I listened to Martin spew his usual remarks about intelligent people, I stared at the crowd and then at the dark foliage of the park. Martin suspected Norman of being an interesting person, intelligent enough to talk to if he could only examine his credentials more closely.

"It's going to rain again," I said stretching my hand out to catch the initial drops.

"Let me say good-bye to Norman," Isabel said. She dashed away, and I lost sight of her in the throng moving toward a covered archway to get out of the rain. Martin and I moved with the crowd. We waited under the archway for what seemed a long time. Isabel returned in a different mood than she had left, Norman having failed to perform his good-bye in the manner she expected. Busy with other people, he had kept her waiting only to dismiss her perfunctorily.

"It serves me right," she said.

We walked into the rain, and the sadness I had seen earlier that day again overwhelmed her.

3

The three of us got together again a few days later at the Delacorte Theater to see *As You Like It*. While waiting on line for the tickets, an all-day affair, I managed to make myself scarce for a while to give Martin an opportunity to make his move.

"She's not interested," Martin later said to me. He took the blow quite well. "She must be interested in you," he said.

"I don't think so."

"No, go ahead and try. Don't hold back on my account."

"I wouldn't do that," I honestly said. "She's never been interested before."

"People change."

"Nah, it's no use," I said ambivalently.

She called, and I saw her again without Martin. We saw each other every day for two weeks. Then, lying down on the grass under the shade of a tree in Central Park, I kissed her. She seemed slightly befuddled, as if a kiss were the one thing in the world to which she didn't know how to respond.

"There are some things one can't philosophize about," she said.

Her words puzzled me, and I interpreted her reaction as the lack of interest I had predicted.

"Let's just be friends," she suggested.

Having expected that to be the outcome, I agreed.

4

In August, Isabel's birthday celebration took place at her mother's house. With the facility of a flame, all evening she moved about enveloped in a floor-length design of red and orange flowers on transparent material. The burning dress, I called it, a blaze that smoldered without consuming her. The leaping flames, the magic fire of translucence, all evening mesmerized me—at one moment concentrated in one spot, the next engulfing the whole house. There was no escape; I stared like a zombie obeying a faraway voice. Everyone was drained of color as if having stepped out of a silent film tinted blue—everyone except Isabel, the bright orange flame.

Enthralled by her image, I automatically became a competitor in a contest of my own devising. Any other guy who went near her was someone to watch out for, someone to outdo at attracting her. I branded Henry Stuart as the main opponent at the moment. Isabel's neighbor since childhood, he had the edge on me. There was nothing I could do about the past. I had to outmaneuver him right then. He looked comfortable, at ease, a constant smile on his face as he hovered about her.

Before Isabel blew out the candles, Mrs. Barron brought out a paper crown and ready to place it on Isabel, Henry Stuart magically appeared between mother and daughter. Isabel proceeded to cut the cake, and as we ate, she crossed the room to stand by me, a sign to everyone, but it failed to convince me. In a few minutes, Henry followed her. I figured he wasn't going to give up easily, but neither was I.

"Tell Mario about your boat," Isabel said putting on her mischievous smile.

"Yes," he said, "I have a boat at the 79th Street Boat Basin."

"Oh, come, be more descriptive."

"Well, it's only a rowboat."

"It's a dinghy!" she exclaimed and laughed, a contagious sound that relaxed Henry and induced him to join in. Yes, she could do

147

that. There was always something in her words, in her attitude, that transformed the ordinary into something else. For the rest of the evening, she stayed close to me.

"It's too late for you to go home now," she said to me after everyone had left. Mrs. Barron had gone to bed. Two college girls boarding for the summer also retired to the room upstairs that had once been Isabel's sister's, who, gone for years, occasionally came home to urge the flight of the other two. "I'll put the quilt out for you in the little room," Isabel said. She brought down the bedding, laid it out on the floor in the alcove by the kitchen. "Good night," she said and lightly kissed me on the lips. She left leaving me surprised and elated. I rolled over on one side and tried to sleep. In a while I heard someone come down the stairs and walk into the room. I discerned her outline.

"Do you mind?" she asked.

"No," I answered smiling in the dark.

She slipped in next to me. I touched her very gently, brushed her eyes with my lips then pressed them against hers, parting them. I ran my hand down her back very slowly, memorizing every detail. I pulled her closer to me.

5

In the morning, we got up before everyone else. Mrs. Barron walked into the kitchen while Isabel and I ate bacon and eggs. She didn't look surprised to see me.

"Good morning," she said. "Are you two doing anything special today?"

"What do you want to do, Mario?" Isabel inquired.

"I don't have any plans," I said.

"I'm going antique hunting," said Mrs. Barron.

"Okay, we'll go with you," Isabel said. "If that's all right with you, Mario?"

"Sure," I said.

Mrs. Barron had waited for both her daughters to grow up before divorcing her husband of twenty-five years who had been unfaithful to her from the first week of their marriage. She overpaid for her mistake, but she survived. "She's amazingly sane after having put up with so much. Don't you think so?" Isabel once asked me. "Yes," I answered, not having observed any signs of insanity in Mrs. Barron, except her being married to the wrong person for twenty-five years.

She had finally freed herself at a time in her life when she was about to be left alone, both of her daughters searching for lives of their own. A quietness peered from Mrs. Barron's eyes then scurried away rustling through the blazing leaves of her autumn, something young and nimble, something shy and distrustful, already acquainted with hunters and with death but still amicable. Mrs. Barron was as young as her daughters, perhaps more so—the daughters had been to more places, read more books, held more opinions; they considered themselves educated, informed and in step with the times. In contrast, their mother seemed innocent.

We went down to Bleecker Street to browse the antique shops. In every other shop we passed, Isabel saw something she considered a necessity for her mother.

"Ah, look at that rocking chair," exclaimed Isabel. "Just what you need, Mama."

"It looks a little rickety, don't you think?" said Mrs. Barron, more interested in looking than in buying. "And the price, look at the price!"

"Oh, Mama, it's worth the price. It's not as if you can't afford it."

"It's very easy to spend," said Mrs. Barron looking to me for support.

"It's a beautiful chair. Don't you think so, Mario?" Isabel said pulling me in the opposite direction.

"It's very nice," I said.

"A bit overpriced, I think," said Mrs. Barron.

"Yes, but not in New York," I said trying to be agreeable but getting bored with looking at antiques, the likelihood of a purchase remote, the conversation the same in every shop.

"Oh wow, look at this!" Isabel had stepped into another room at the rear of the shop. "You have to buy this. It'll be great in the kitchen." She was examining a large cabinet contraption equipped with sliding panels and compartments.

"It couldn't be used any other place but the kitchen," said Mrs. Barron.

"What is it?" I inquired.

"Something for bakers. See, here is a place to store the flour. This pulls out and enlarges the work area, very handy."

"It's very nice looking," I said.

But the price offended Mrs. Barron, as if antique dealers had conspired to ask exorbitant prices to pique her, an outrage. She looked puzzled and hurt that her daughter didn't immediately agree.

"That's slightly too high, but it would be great to have. Come on, Mama! Spend some money. That's what it's for."

"Oh, Isabel," she blazed as if a match had been dropped on the stuffing of an old cushion, "that's too big. Where would I put it? There's no room in the kitchen." She had too long accepted being a victim to feel comfortable defending herself against anybody, but she had resolved to do herself justice. But losing her temper at the moment revived a feeling of guilt about the outcome of her daughter's upbringing.

On Macdougal Street, we sat down at a café, the interior of the place dark and the coffee overpriced. All the waiters wore white shirts and red jackets.

"I did the best I could," Mrs. Barron said directing the remark at me, although there was no need to so. I had already credited her with good intentions and willingly granted that she had performed a remarkable feat. However, she still doubted her success.

"It's not your fault, Mama. It's nobody's fault."

"I did you a great wrong by staying married to him for so long."

"Mama, it's done. It's over—"

I observed the waiters glide about, then I turned my head to look through the front window as a teenage girl strolled by tightly packaged in her blue jeans. My eyes followed her until she disappeared beyond the shop window.

"That's the only thing I regret that you and Karen were hurt. I tried to leave him once," she turned to me again. "I took the two girls and went to a hotel. Isabel was only eight then."

"And he found you?"

"I left a note," Isabel contritely admitted.

Silence reigned for a moment, and then Mrs. Barron continued, her voice more cheerful, as if the topic had changed, "For a long time I didn't know how he found us so quickly."

"Karen knew about the note, but she promised not to tell. She wouldn't have left a note, though. I betrayed you." Isabel held back her tears.

"That was a long time ago—a long time ago."

I had put too much sugar in my coffee, and I reluctantly sipped the liquid.

"He's such a bastard—such a bastard," intoned Mrs. Barron shaking her head.

"Oh, Mama, let's forget it. It's over. It's over." Tears streaked down her cheeks.

"That's the trouble with my girl. She's too sensitive. Once, when she was still in a stroller, I was out shopping with her and Karen. I didn't want to cross the street with both children and the packages, so I took Karen first and left Isabel at the curb. She must have thought I was leaving her behind for good. She became very upset and threw up, right there, all over herself."

"Now you consider me sensitive; you used to think I was retarded when I was little; I was so moody."

"Oh, Isabel, I never thought that, never!" Mrs. Barron turned her head to look through the window. I expected to see tears streak down her face also, but she drove to the edge and stopped.

After the café, Mrs. Barron chose to return uptown. Isabel and I decided to roam about the Village a while longer. Mother and daughter kissed before parting. They held each other tightly—a reaffirmation of a bond above duty and respect, a bond contracted under duress. They had lived for so long with a common enemy that the relationship of mother and daughter had been transformed into that of allies, woman to woman, a friendship to be nurtured like a luxuriant flower growing through a crack in the sidewalk. Caught by an invisible mesh that gently pulled me in a direction I had not anticipated, an unfamiliar path I consequently feared, I uneasily observed the solicitude between mother and daughter.

Mrs. Barron kissed me also. The embrace vaguely bound me to a promise. I had taken a first step, and I was forced to take another in order to keep my balance. The first step was long in coming. I preferred quick steps. This one I found hard to judge accurately. It covered much ground, and for all the time elapsed it may have been too quick. Only recently she had said, "Ah, so you're Mario. I'm pleased to meet you—no longer a voice on the telephone." She had looked at me intently, sized me up, compared me to the image she had constructed using my voice as Adam's rib had been used. She had blown life into that image, had invested in it, and I, on hearing her words, knew that she had assigned a value to it. Confused for a moment, somewhat flattered, I glimpsed the process about to be used on the clay provided by my presence. I felt taken up and, though not adverse to that in general, imputing no malice to her, I became uncomfortably aware of some arrangement, a kind I had never previously accepted.

Mrs. Barron disappeared into the subway, and Isabel and I, again confronted with each other, went to see a movie. *Joanne Woodward plays a teacher whose life is slipping by uneventfully. She decides to do something about it. The seduction scene takes place in the woods. The guy takes a blanket out of the car. They walk to a small clearing. He spreads the blanket on the ground. She takes her dress off. She's awkward. It's her first time. She cries.* I turned to look at Isabel, tears in her eyes.

6

Isabel moved to a one-room apartment on Eighty-third Street, right off Central Park West. Not much space, but she was happy to move in. She took childhood objects and memories to her new abode. Things others try to leave behind she made an effort to take with her. Instead of looking forward to the creation of something new, she was out to regain something lost.

Shortly after her move, she stayed at my place for several days.

On the third morning, she announced, "I'm leaving, and I'm not coming back. I can't do this."

I stood rooted on the spot, trying to maintain a semblance of composure. She looked at me intently with a determination to stand by her decision.

"This relationship has to end," she said. "I have to leave. It's for your own good as well as mine."

"How is it for my good?"

"There's something wrong with me. Can't you see? I'm not good for you. I'm not all here for you. You deserve somebody who will be with you."

"I don't understand this," I said.

"I don't understand it either. I only know that I have to leave."

"You don't have to. You want to."

"Don't make it hard for me," she pleaded. "I love you, I do."

I followed her out into the hall and watched her descend the stairs.

"Are you sure of what you're doing?" I shouted after her.

"I'm sure," she said without turning.

I stood there until I could no longer hear the sound of her footsteps.

A few hours later the phone rang. Her voice at the other end, "I have to explain this to you."

"You don't owe me anything," I said, "not even an explanation."

"You have the wrong idea of why I left. I don't want you to think badly of me. I have to explain."

"I'm listening."

"I can't do it on the phone. Come to dinner tomorrow."

"Okay," I said.

When I got there, I stifled the urge to walk out. She had invited another couple. I assumed a semblance of composure. Isabel transformed her discomfort into hostility exhibited in wit no less brutal for its virtuosity. She directed her venom at the unfortunate guests who, not knowing what they had gotten themselves into, had the good sense to depart as soon as politeness allowed. Genuinely moved by their plight, I gladly saw them leave for their sake as well as mine.

"Why the hell did you invite them? I thought this was going to be a *tête-à-tête* between us."

"I don't know why. Before I realized what I was doing, the words were out of my mouth. I thought you wouldn't mind too much since he's an acquaintance of yours."

"Before today, I had spoken to him only once in my life."

"Well, he said he was your friend. I didn't know he was going to bring her along."

"You mean it was going to be just the three of us for dinner?"

"No, I invited Henry Stuart too, but he didn't show up."

"Jesus Christ! What were you trying to do? If you wanted to avoid talking to me, all you had to do was tell me not to come. I wouldn't have insisted."

"Don't shout at me."

"And did you have to be nasty to them besides? Why?"

"I don't know; I don't know. You made me nervous."

I suppressed the urge to make an exit.

"Well, here we are," I said.

"Yes, here we are," she echoed. "Don't be unkind to me. We have to work something out," she continued. "It didn't seem right the way we parted the other day."

She launched into an explanation. She talked for what seemed to me a long time, but her words failed to clarify what she was trying to explain.

"You just want us to be friends and nothing else?" I asked, trying to extract a simple proposition, something I could deal with on my own terms.

"We've gone a little too far for that, haven't we?" she conceded.

"I'd say so, but what then?"

"I don't know exactly."

"Well, this is where we were before I arrived this evening."

"No, I wanted you to know that I love you."

"We can call each other sometimes," I said, "when we get lonely."

"You're not going to call me ever, are you?"

"Maybe I will," I said.

"I don't want it to end this way."

"How, then?"

"Don't be angry," she pleaded. "It's late already, stay tonight."

7

"I don't believe you haven't painted this apartment," she said to me right after she moved in.

"It doesn't need painting. It's clean."

"But it's ugly."

"Well, we can paint it if you want."

So we started our life together with a coat of paint. There are magical moments that can't be discounted. They become imprinted in one's memory, like that moment in the library when I first became enthralled by her image. Why such moments become so enchanted, I cannot say. It's a wonder of the human psyche. It attaches significance to acquired images in order to project itself into the physical world.

At the Door Store we purchased chairs, a three-legged design, the seat a triangle retreating to the backrest. They were small enough for us to lug home on our own.

"Are you sure you want to do this?"

"We can manage," Isabel said.

Before we reached West 4th Street, I noticed blood on Isabel's left heel.

"You're bleeding," I said.

She looked down at the sandaled foot to see the blood.

"It must've been a piece of glass."

"I didn't feel it," she said putting down the chairs.

"Sit down," I said. Pulling a handkerchief from my pocket, I knelt to wipe the blood and examine the wound.

"It's not much," she said.

"Oh, it's a cut," I said.

"We have to get home."

"I'll take two chairs home and come back for you and the other two."

"That's silly," she said. "I can manage."

"Are you sure?"

"Certainly, I'm sure."

"Let me tie the handkerchief around your heel."

"That'll make it harder for me to walk."

"Well, then let me hold it here until you stop bleeding."

Passers-by glanced at us occasionally, but no one stopped or said anything, and we too ignored everything else going on in the street.

The moment absorbed me. The need to take care of her transported me to a magical place.

Other incidents had an opposite effect—small things that made me wonder what transpired behind her unfathomable façade.

"I think we should take fencing lessons," she one day said.

I looked up from my notebook. I had been trying write a paragraph about the clay that had surrounded the house I lived in as a child.

"That's what I want to do," she said. "We can do that together, take lessons and everything."

"Fencing," I said, still thinking about the red clay.

"Yes, fencing," Isabel said. "You know, with foils and everything."

"Yes, fine," I said.

I assumed that she would arrange for the lessons, but a few weeks later she again brought up the subject.

"Well, have you looked into it and made arrangements?" I asked.

"First buy the foils. That'll get me going."

"Buy foils?"

"Sure," she said. "That's no big deal. I want to do this, but I need something to get me going."

"But once I buy them, you'll take over from there?"

"Yes, of course," she said.

I looked in the Yellow Pages to find a place that sold fencing equipment. A few days later, I arrived home carrying the package.

"Here they are," I said to Isabel as I placed the box on the kitchen table.

"What have you got in there?" she asked glancing up from her task.

Needle and thread in hand, she was altering a skirt. I wondered how fencing fit into the scheme, but I saw no point in inquiring. I opened the package to reveal the contents.

"Ah, very good," she said and, without moving from her seat, she continued sewing.

"I got them for you."

"For us, yes," she corrected me.

"Don't you want to see how they feel?"

"I will," she said without looking up.

Trying to control my annoyance, I left the package on the table and walked out and down to the street. I proceeded all the way to Bleecker and then back. On returning, the package had been removed from the table, and Isabel stood by the stove sautéing vegetables.

"Homemade Chinese food," she said. "You'll like it."

Yes, I knew I would. I knew also that the foils would not be mentioned again or retrieved from wherever she had stored them.

We oscillated between moments of joy and stretches of misery. Eventually, I suggested she get a job.

"Why?"

"Because that'll keep you from moping around all day. Doing nothing isn't good for you."

"I'd work if I could."

"You've got to do something. Maybe you can go to school."

"Maybe," she said.

"You can't go on like this for the rest of your life."

"I know," she said, "I know. I thought you would save me," she said more than once.

My moment had come, but there was nothing I could do but retreat into platitude. "No one can save anybody else," I said. "Each must save himself."

"You're right," she answered with a smile. "You're right."

She returned to her silence. Seemingly calm, I resumed my walk around the fortress, refusing to accept the inevitable, catching only glimpses of what she might be. Sometimes she came to life more a sprite than a woman.

My leaving for work every morning became an issue. "Don't go today," she said holding on to me as I tried to free myself from the sheets.

"It's hard enough to get up without you holding me down," I retorted. "Please let me go."

"Please stay."

"If I don't work, how will we pay the rent?"

"We'll manage," she said.

8

I arrived at the San Francisco airport tired, having missed the early flight and spending most of the day at O'Hare. I had been in Wisconsin for a couple of weeks with a woman whom I had met at a poetry reading. She was a New Yorker, but she had bought a farm in Wisconsin after having fallen in love with the topography of the Midwest. The house was her summer place. She leased the fields to a local farmer.

More than two months had passed since I had last seen Isabel. She had gone to San Francisco ostensibly to visit her sister. She had left all her belongings, and of course, I expected her to return. We spoke on the phone, but in those conversations she never explained anything. She never said that she wasn't returning, but she never had immediate plans to do so. She wrote vague letters and postcards of her own design; my favorite a cartoon of a princess trapped in a tower. The dialogue balloon held the words, "Forgive me." For what, I wondered, but figuring that art always expressed some truth, I had something on which to base my hopes. Riding to her rescue, I looked forward to the reunion when everything would be all right again.

I had not been waiting long when I saw her step out of the car. She ran to throw her arms around me.

"I'm glad to see you," she said.

An auspicious beginning, my doubts disappeared.

"Were you waiting long?" she asked. "I went by the departure gate first thinking I had given you the wrong instructions."

"No, this is exactly where you said you'd meet me."

"I'm glad to see you," she repeated, her smile overwhelming her face once again.

I tossed my backpack on the back seat, and we drove into the city, a short ride.

"My sister is away for the week," she said. "So we'll have the apartment to ourselves."

Yes, the stars were on my side for a change. "I missed you a lot," I said.

"Same here," she said. After a long silence, she continued, "You look tired."

"Long trip."

"From Wisconsin, you said?"

"Yes," I answered failing to elaborate.

"We don't have to talk about it," she said.

I would tell her everything, but I would just as well wait. The phone rang as we got to the second-floor apartment in the three-story house on a typically slanted street in San Francisco. "Ah, yes, I meant to call you," Isabel said having picked up the phone. "I can't see you tomorrow." For a moment she moved the receiver away from her ear. "Don't be upset," she said to the person at the other end. "Mario is here, so my time is taken at the moment." Isabel grimaced as she looked at me while still listening to the voice at the other end. "I'll call you when I get a chance." She hung up, then turning to me she explained, "That was a friend, Hillary. We had tentative plans to get together tomorrow, and she's upset that I've cancelled."

"She's angry?"

"Quite," Isabel said. "You must be hungry. Let me fix you something to eat."

I stood there quietly wondering whether I had just been signaled to drop the subject.

"A hot bath will relax you," she said. She appreciated bodily comfort, something I habitually ignored, as if my body did not exist except in the proximity of a woman. She got the warm water flowing and came to fetch me, led me by the hand to the bathroom and began to unbutton my shirt.

"I can do that," I said.

"I know," she said. "I've missed you."

I wondered whether I was the one who had walked away and who now had returned. I stepped into the warm water and sat down to gaze at her as she undressed as if for the first time revealing to me the lines

160

of her body. My eyes followed, sliding down from her breasts to her hips and along her thighs all the way to her feet. She had lost weight since I had last seen her.

"You've gotten smaller," I said as she stepped into the tub to sit facing me, her legs entwining mine.

"My breasts are too small for you?" The pique in her voice startled me.

"I only meant you lost weight, that's all," I said, my tone pleading for mercy.

Indeed, I had neglected the art of saying only what others wanted to hear, but this time I was simply misunderstood. She too, trying to do her best, let the brief outburst subside, again smiling, as if the moment had been imaginary. We contemplated each other as we had that first week when she had moved in at Renwick Street. The months of turmoil before she left for San Francisco seemed a nightmare from which we were now awakening.

"What were you doing in Wisconsin?" she asked.

I stared blankly into her eyes searching for a reply or perhaps merely conveying one without words.

"I went there with an acquaintance," I said.

"A woman?"

"Yes."

"You're in love with her?"

"No," I truthfully said.

"But you went to bed with her."

"Yes," I squirmed.

9

"Sure," she said into the phone, "come on over and meet Mario." After hanging up she explained, "That was Larry Lessing, a friend of my sister's. He's just on his way home from a hiking trip. He thought he'd stop by and say hello."

"Here first before going home to drop off his backpack?"

161

"Well, this is on his way home. No big deal. I suppose he expected Karen to be here."

"But she's not, and he's going to drop by anyway?"

"He wants to meet you," she said. "He's heard a lot about you."

"Has he? I suppose Karen talks about me all the time."

"I suppose she does."

Larry Lessing arrived, a bottle of wine in hand. Slim and tall, topped with a mass of dark curly hair, he sported a constant smile. Handing Isabel the bottle, he placed his backpack on the floor by the front door.

"Show Mario the backpack," Isabel said.

"Why don't we have some wine first," Larry suggested.

"Larry designed the backpack himself," Isabel said, a glee in her voice. "See, the frame is made of plastic tubing and can be easily disassembled. Larry invented it; a great idea, don't you think?"

"I suppose it is," I said, though I generally didn't attribute much importance to backpack frames. On the other hand, the paper clip had been quite an invention, and perhaps a plastic backpack frame would eventually become as common, an everyday object, life without one unimaginable.

"I bet Mario wants to drink some wine," Larry said.

"Sounds like you're the one who wants a drink," Isabel countered as she searched through a kitchen drawer for the corkscrew.

"I certainly do," Larry said.

I sat down in the armchair and he on the couch facing me. In the kitchen, Isabel uncorked the wine. On a tray, she brought the bottle and the glasses into the living room and placed them on the coffee table. She poured the wine and passed a glass to each of us. Holding her own wineglass, she stood by the table as if trying to decide where to sit, then said, "There's too much light in this room," and proceeded to turn off the overhead. Then, only a small lamp behind the sofa provided light. She sat on the floor by me, leaning on my right leg.

"On the floor?" Larry said. "There are plenty of more comfortable places."

"I'm comfy enough," Isabel assured him.

A vague feeling of discomfort overwhelmed me as I sensed something, but exactly what escaped me.

10

I soon had enough of San Francisco, tired of the hills, the fog, the lack of bustle; every movie playing in town had already played in New York weeks before. Trolley cars had no appeal. Why did she want to be in this town if not to get away from me? The park with the false ruins, a monument to schlock, the whole city on a geological fault waiting for the inevitable, perhaps a good reason for avoiding erecting anything of aesthetic value. *Yesterday* reverberated through my head, *love was such an easy game to play*, exactly what I felt, *a place to hide away*, what I needed; yes, I believed in yesterday.

While she attended art class, I waited for her in the small park on a hilltop. I leaned over the stone fence and gazed down the hill to see her ascending from the street. Yes, she was different even in the simple brown dress, a statement of elegance that constantly overwhelmed me, an ideal beyond explanation, beyond reason. I watched her approach. She suddenly raised her eyes to meet mine; her lips broke into that enigmatic smile, the interpretation again left up to me. When she got to the top of the hill we embraced.

"What shall we do today?" she asked in her distinctive voice, a natural but mysterious accent from which no one would have ever guessed that she grew up in the Bronx.

"Let's just sit here for a while," I said letting my back slide down the stone wall.

She sat next to me, still smiling, as if I had chosen exactly the ideal pastime, her body close to mine, trying to blur the natural boundary. I wondered whether ambiguity would ever cease, whether she would forever hold on to me while simultaneously rejecting me.

"You know why I came to San Francisco."

"To see me."

"Not just to see you."

"I can't go back yet. For your own good as well as mine. But I shouldn't even say it that way. I love you, but I won't pretend to be doing anything for your benefit. I don't know who I am, and that's what I have to find out."

"Do I keep you from doing that?"

"It's not anything you do or don't do. My problems are not your fault. I've been telling you that from the beginning."

"We all have to find ourselves, but we don't do it alone. We do it in each other's company. How else can we determine boundaries?"

"I'm so lost, I need time by myself."

"All right, I'll wait for you."

"It would be unfair of me to ask that of you. I don't know who I'll be or where I'll be eventually."

More to the conversation than words, she pulled one knee up toward her chin, the short skirt of her dress sliding down her thigh to reveal her one undergarment. I raised my eyes to hers, and she smiled, this time with a clear meaning. Her body she would not deny me for the moment. My discomfort at being offered only that surprised me, as if I had forgotten all the other women I had known, all somewhere else now, along with a myriad of others ready to take their place.

"And after that, what then? Home alone?"

The humor rose to her eyes in the familiar look of incisive wit that constantly perked in her. And I, sorry to let my maudlin state expose me to the barbs I had always watched her hurl at others, waited for her to remind me of Wisconsin. But she restrained herself, suppressing the instinctive urge to hurl her barbs; she let another side emerge, always a woman's reflex to protect the ones she loves. "Aren't some of your friends going down to Mexico? Why don't you go with them? Have a good time."

"I'll go if you come along."

"I have to stay here until my sister gets back, and the summer course at the art school is still going. You go meet your friends, and I'll see if I can get down there in a week or so. I promise I'll go if I can. And anyway you can have a good time at the carnival without me. Your friends will be there."

She had never liked my friends. She magnified their faults and quirks. "Can't you see what they're like?" she once asked me. Of course I saw who they were, but I wasn't much different from them. She had surely observed my faults just as clearly as everyone else's. That realization filled me with fear that she had no more reason to be with me than with any of them.

Back in our college days, she had avoided mingling with my friends; she always stayed in the east wing of the cafeteria while my friends and I hung out at the opposite end of Finley. Perhaps that had been just as well. Her difference attracted me, my view all summed up in that ethereal image etched on my consciousness that day in the library when I had seen her enveloped in the light of the afternoon sun.

"I would be going down there just to wait for you," I said.

"I'll try," she said. "But you should go for the carnival. You'll have a good time."

11

On my way down to the border, I got to San Diego in the morning, but the Greyhound bus wasn't scheduled to leave until three o'clock. So I spent the day wandering about downtown. I looked in the windows of several bars advertising topless dancers, but on a Sunday morning there was nothing going on. Now and then, sailors walked by seemingly engaged in the same pastime. A blond with a beehive hairdo and a tight leather skirt that scarcely covered her thighs approached me. I declined. She waited for a sailor.

Down by the bay, warships dominated the docks. I thought of my cousin Manuel who was in Vietnam. After having been arrested for some shenanigan, the judge gave Manuel a choice: join up or go to jail. He joined the marines. He sent home pictures of himself in full dress uniform, and everyone was proud of him.

When we were children in Puerto Rico, Manuel lived in the mountains, and I lived closer to the sea. We were together only sometimes when my family went to the mountains to visit. The town had only one street that ran through the flat part of the town and down by the square where the church stood guard at one end. Most of the houses were on the hillsides on either side of the road, poised as if to slide down, one on top of the other, right into the square and the church. A river cascaded down from the mountain and ran by the town for a stretch parallel to the road. On the winding road with a sheer drop on one side, I rode up from the city with my father in a public car. Often we saw the wrecks of cars that had gone over the edge.

One time, coming home from another war in the Orient, a soldier rode in the car with us. He was returning from a war that could not be won, just like the war that Manuel was in could not be won. Wanting to surprise his wife, the soldier was arriving home unannounced. As the car approached his house, we saw the young woman in the backyard hanging the wash on the clothesline. The soldier got out and knocked at the door. We waited eager to see the reunion. The young woman approached the door. When she saw her husband, she was momentarily paralyzed; then, she threw her arms around his neck and hung on to him. In the car, everyone smiled, happy to see them together again though we had never seen either one of them before.

The car drove on up the winding road to Naranjito. At the square, we got out and walked down an alley, past the grocery store and across the river on a plank bridge. We walked up the mountain on the dirt road. Up there, Manuel and I went fishing for catfish, and we climbed trees to look at the eggs in the bird nests. We kept from touching them so the mother bird would not reject them. Those were fun things to do, fishing and climbing trees, and picking guavas and mangos off the trees. And we peeled a little bark from the banana trees, the bark brown like dry tobacco; we rolled it up into make-believe cigars and pretended to smoke.

But banana bark didn't smell like tobacco, so we went to Don Pedro's tobacco barn where the leaves hung to dry, and the air was heavy with the smell of tobacco. We peeked into the cavernous building and took deep breaths, but we never walked in under the drying leaves, though we wanted to, afraid that Don Pedro would come by and chase us away. We were very casual when we walked by his barn, and Don Pedro never said anything but *"Buenos días, señoritos."* We raised the tip of our fingers to our eyebrows in a casual salute as if we were his equals. The gentleman took it in stride and only turned away to tend to his business.

Now Manuel was gone off to a war—to kill or to be killed, and I was on my way to Mexico to meet my friends and have a holiday but mostly to wait for Isabel.

At three o'clock I got on the bus. There was not much to see out the window on the way to the border. Southern California is a dry place; everywhere the stunted trees are surrounded by brown grass. The bus arrived at Mexicali by six o'clock. At the border station, I declared how much money I had. I lied as I had been instructed. The border guard flipped through the book of traveler's checks and handed it back to me. He didn't care whether I had stated the correct amount. A ponderous man with a thick black moustache and an unctuous, somewhat repulsive look, he asked me where I was going. I told him.

"The train leaves at seven o'clock," the guard said.

"I'll take the next one," I rejoined. He looked at me quizzically. *"Buenas noches,"* I said, and I walked off. The border station might have had a sign that read, *"Despair all ye who enter here,"* but I didn't notice it.

A local urchin directed me to a fleabag hotel, fifty pesos for the night, about four American dollars. After breakfast the next day, I headed out to the train station, a ways out of town. When I got there, I realized why the border guard had informed me of the time of departure. The train ran every twenty-four hours. There wouldn't be another train till the evening. It was dawning on me that although I was only a few miles from California, life was very different here. There was not much else to do but hang out at the terminal till the next train. The ticket office wouldn't open till about three o'clock.

I retrieved *One Hundred Years of Solitude* from my backpack and read for a while to pass the time. About noon I got hungry. A luncheonette occupied one end of the station. I sat at the counter and ordered pork chops with rice and beans. On a television behind the counter, a soap opera played. After lunch, I retreated to the benches at the center of the station. I tried to start up a conversation with two Canadian girls who also had arrived to wait for the train, but they seemed reticent to talk to a stranger. Perhaps they took me for a *bandido* although I wasn't wearing a six-shooter or even a sombrero. Their fear would keep them from enjoying their trip. At three o'clock, the ticket office opened for business, and I was confronted with another unexpected choice: first class, second class, third class, or Pullman? I figured Pullman was the sleeping car, and I didn't need to lie down to sleep. I bought a first-class ticket thinking to treat myself to a comfortable ride.

As departure time approached, the station became crowded. Hundreds of Mexican peasants sprung from the ground to ride the train. They carried beat-up valises, baskets, or just tied-up bundles. I had not thought it necessary to rush on board for first class. I had assumed that nomenclature corresponded to some privileges. All those Indians will probably be riding second and third class, I thought. I expected to walk into first class to see ladies and gentlemen in their Sunday best sitting in clean comfortable seats.

I was soon disabused. There was great commotion and disorder in the car. Everyone tried to accommodate their bundles the best they could. Most of the seats were already taken, and many passengers were resigned to standing passage. Those still hoping to be seated moved down the aisle looking for any possible accommodation. A woman who seemed to be reserving the seat next to her for someone asked me whether I wanted to sit. I accepted her offer, and she happily moved her bundles to make way for me.

On the map, I had calculated the trip to be about four hundred miles. I figured the train could easily travel at eighty miles an hour. With a few hours for stops and whatnot, I figured a seven-to-eight hour trip would put me at my destination by early morning. For a while, I conversed with the woman next to me. She was pleasant and outgoing for a stranger on a train. That was unusual, but she was otherwise uninteresting. She probably thought the same about me. After a while, she decided to sleep. I wished to do the same, but I wasn't sleepy.

The night darkness obscured the landscape. Once in a while there were lights in some ghostly hamlet or solitary rancho, maybe a cantina along the tracks was open late. But mostly, all I saw were the dark and irregular shapes of desert vegetation and geological formations. After a few hours of travel, I realized that my estimate of how long I would be on the train was rather off. A man on a bicycle could have easily kept pace with the train. I dozed off eventually only to be awakened just before dawn by the cries of the conductor announcing the next stop and by the commotion of people preparing to get off.

There were soldiers on the platform when the train pulled in. From my seat, I couldn't see what was going on, but I surmised that people were being searched as they got off the train. After they had searched the people getting off, the soldiers—combat rifles slung on their shoulders—came aboard. Three soldiers boarded at each end of the car, one stayed by the door. The other two proceeded down the aisle randomly selecting baggage to search.

The passengers complied without a word. All faces were similarly configured in a serious expression that failed to reveal anything but resignation to an annoying but unavoidable routine. The soldiers too had a fixed expression of stern authority that ill fitted their youthful faces. A man across the aisle from me was ordered to open the bundle that lay at his feet. He obeyed with studied deliberateness.

The soldier stood but a few inches away from me. I looked up at his face. He had the complexion of a child—had never shaved. The machine gun, an encumbrance, hung from his shoulder. The gun was made of very dark metal, and the barrel had holes. That's to reduce the heat, I reasoned as I imagined the weapon spitting bullets.

At the third stop, I was asked to open my luggage. By that time, having gotten used to the routine, I assumed the role of observer at my own search. I wondered what these soldiers were looking for. I had never heard of any great smuggling traffic from the U.S. into Mexico.

I turned to the woman next to me, and I asked her what she thought they were looking for.

"Guns," she said. "There are many bandits in this part of the country, and sometimes they travel on the train."

She said that matter-of-factly as if bandits and soldiers were an everyday phenomenon. I refrained from asking any more questions.

The morning light transformed everything. The desert was more awesome than I had expected. Actually, I had not expected anything nor actively imagined what kind of terrain I was traversing. If anything, I expected a continuation of the California landscape, less than lush but at least a recognizable shade of green. Now, the desert sun was unrelenting, and the colors were all reds and yellows with a dash of magenta thrown in here and there. To my amazement, we occasionally passed by small herds of cattle wandering about in a cactus forest. I wondered what they survived on. The cactus didn't seem at all appetizing. But no doubt, cattle, like people, make do with what's available.

Surprisingly, my traveling companion looked much better in the bright sunlight than she had in the evening's light. Her age was difficult to determine, but I had thought her considerably older than she now appeared. She was possibly younger than I. Perhaps being more relaxed once the train ride had settled into a predictable routine, I was more receptive; or because she was traveling alone, at first she had assumed an unprepossessing aura for her own protection, and having concluded that I was a reliable character, she relaxed her guard. She had a dark complexion, dark eyes and hair typical of the native population, but her long face and sharp features revealed a European strain.

She was returning to a small town not far from Guaymas, where I was headed.

"Are you going there for the festival?" she asked.

"Yes, I am," I replied. "So you know about the festival?"

"Yes, of course, everyone knows about the festival. It is a very big event in these parts. It is the biggest festival in the state of Sonora, perhaps the biggest festival in all of Mexico. That's what some people say, but I don't know since I haven't been to any others. But even you, a foreigner, have heard of this one."

As we had been speaking in Spanish, I asked her how she knew I was a foreigner.

"I know by your accent."

"I could be from Mexico City."

"I don't know where you're from, but you're not Mexican."

"Did you know I was a foreigner when you asked me to sit down?"

"I wasn't sure. Your clothing and your baggage are like an American, but your Spanish sounds natural, so you must be from somewhere else."

I waited a moment for her to ask me were I was from, but she didn't.

I looked into her eyes. She leaned back against the window, the corners of her mouth turned up in a coquettish grin. She seemed at that moment very exotic. I imagined that she would ask me to get off the train with her. Would I, if she did? I didn't know anything about her. She might be married or divorced; might live with her parents and ten brothers and sisters or maybe with an old maiden aunt whom she looked after—all possibilities.

I imagined her asking me to go with her. She would surely have all the details worked out. All I would have to do would be to follow her instructions. Perhaps she would ask me to meet her at some clandestine place in the evening. I would wait all day to spend a few hours in the evening with her while the town slept, and I would continue my journey the next day.

The train lurched on toward its destination. At the next stop, a small army of vendors invaded the cars with all sorts of goods. I bought ham and cheese sandwiches for my companion and myself and also Pepsi Colas. My companion's name was Margarita De Santos. She lived in Camuy, a village not far from Guaymas. She had been in Mexicali to visit a sick aunt. She was returning to her grandparents with whom she had lived since the death of her father and mother in a cholera epidemic.

"I will get off soon," she said. She seemed to be waiting for me to respond to that announcement, but I didn't say anything. "Enjoy the fiesta," she said.

"Yes, thank you. Perhaps you will be there?"

"Perhaps," she replied, "but probably not."

"I hope you will make it. It will be fun."

As the train screeched to a halt, she gathered her bundles. "Well, good-bye," she said.

She had been sitting on the inside, so I got up to let her out. I kept my eyes on her as she moved toward the exit. She didn't turn to look back. Laden with her bundles, she descended from the car and moved along the platform away from me. I watched her through the window until she turned at the corner of the building.

I kept staring at the deserted railway platform until an image came up. In high school, I had been in love with Annie Camper, the president of the literary club. I had plowed through the pages of *The Magic Mountain*, the only way I could spend time with her, be in the same room with her, talk to her. But that was all. We lived in different worlds that touched only in school, in the literary club where we could discuss the complexities of Thomas Mann.

A social barrier kept reality from interfering and preserved my image of her. I had loved her during the three high school years after which we parted, she going away to an out-of-town college, but soon returning with an ailment that would take her away forever. A memory persisted of sitting with her in the Finley Hall cafeteria, she more subdued than usual and I trying to keep my eyes from the dark blotches on her arms.

When the illness progressed to where she could no longer attend school, I wrote to her, telling her that I loved her. She wrote back thanking me for my expression of kindness. But I saw no kindness in my feelings or in my revelation of them. A process beyond my control ran its course, revealed to me as I sat in the darkness of a theater watching *Yesterday, Today and Tomorrow*, Sophia Loren's image transformed into Annie's.

The train moved on. I arrived at the Guaymas station just about three o'clock—eighteen hours after I had boarded in Mexicali. Everything was dry and dusty, including my mouth. I looked around for signs of civilization; but other than the train station, there was nothing around but the road through the desert. Several public cars were parked near the station, their drivers drumming up business from the disembarking passengers. Most of the cars had hand-lettered signs on the windshield indicating their destination. I headed toward a car with a Guaymas sign on it. There were other customers in the car already, and I made a full complement. In relation to the train ride, the trip into town was short. There were no other vehicles on the road, but we stopped several times to let out passengers. I was the only one riding all the way into town. The car took me straight to the hotel, El Leon de Oro.

12

In the middle of downtown Guaymas, El Leon de Oro Hotel occupied more frontage than any other structure on the south side of the street. Its days of glory long gone, its state of shabbiness provided a friendly familiarity appreciated by those less than comfortable in a foreign place. It was constructed in the Latin style; the rooms around an atrium, the veranda on the second level overlooked the center courtyard. There had to be some merit in staying at such a picturesque hotel, but for the life of me, I couldn't think of it.

Don Gregorio, the desk clerk, short, bald, with a rather reddish complexion, had eyes like a small animal. He gazed steadily evaluating intentions and giving the impression that he would bolt at the slightest threat. Reflexively, anyone observing assumed the most unmenacing attitude as when coaxing a squirrel to accept peanuts from a human hand. I inquired after my friends.

"Ah, you must be Señor Ortega," Don Gregorio said dropping his guard. "Your friends have arranged everything. A good thing for you sir, otherwise we would have turned you away, all booked for the fiesta, as you know."

"Yes, thank you," I said. "A room with a shower I hope."

"Of course, of course!"

"I'll go up then, because I need to use it."

The room—upstairs front, with two beds, a dresser, and a built-in closet—was spacious and clean but drab. It overlooked the street. In the completely tiled bathroom, the shower area consisted of a square indentation on the floor with a drain slightly off center and a nozzle sticking out of the wall. A large water bug crawled across the floor. I stepped on it carefully to avoid crushing it completely, then picking it up with a piece of tissue, I flushed it down the toilet. The accommodations less than luxurious were adequate enough. After washing up and dressing, I went down to the lobby. Don Gregorio had no idea where the "Americans" had gone or when they would return, so I ventured out to explore a little on my own, scouting for the various key establishments—restaurants and bars.

On my return, noting Don Gregorio inclining his head toward the courtyard, I looked in that direction and was gratified to see Martin sitting in a most uncomfortable-looking chair and reading the *New York Times*. On hearing my footsteps, Martin looked up and immediately on his feet made an animated, if not altogether graceful, dash to greet me. The genuine expression of goodwill on his rugged face made his approach more than welcomed. We exchanged the usual chitchat about the journey and its novelty. Martin, having arrived two days before, was full of tidbits of information and speculations about the place. I quickly became impatient fearing a barrage of details about the town when I merely wanted to know the whereabouts of the rest of the crew.

"Where have you managed to lose the others?"

Martin thought for a moment as if trying to figure out what others I was talking about. "They went down to Cuernavaca for the day," he finally said, "and the night. They won't be back till tomorrow," he added as if an afterthought.

Martin tensed assuming responsibility for the look of disappointment that invaded me, but he quickly recovered—tried to cheer me up. "We can look around town much better without them, just like in the old days, when you and I searched for new worlds to conquer."

I smiled. The old days, indeed not so long ago, had been sort of fun, with only some chagrin here and there.

"Did you notice right next door there's a little café and discothèque where all the young people of this town hang out? There are some good-looking *señoritas* here, let me tell you."

"Good-looking *señoritas* that hang out in discothèques like these can land us in a lot of trouble. This is not the good old US of A."

"Don't be an old hen. I already checked out the place. They love Americans here."

"Do they?"

"Sure, they do."

"Well, you'll pass for an American."

Martin ignored my awful mood. He pulled one of the clunky chairs across the tiled patio, no mean feat given the weight of the iron chair, but we had now two side by side, and we continued our conversation sitting down.

"So what do you think of the hotel? It's the real thing, not like those glass tourist traps," Martin said. "This is it, the real thing."

"And what, pray tell, is the measure of reality here?"

Martin thought about that for a minute. His words implied a criterion, a novel idea that he had yet to clarify to himself. "Yes," he said, "I see what you mean. This building seems historical, a traditionally Mexican building, you know, Spanish architecture and all that. This is an atrium we're in. This style goes back to the Romans."

"Yes, I suppose it does. It's kind of cozy to be sitting in the middle of ancient history."

"That's what I mean," Martin seriously said.

"Listen, what are we going to do for dinner?" I asked to change the subject. I didn't want to laugh at Martin's expense, though perhaps he wanted me to. I wasn't sure of anything at the moment.

"I think we should be adventuresome and try something different."

"Well, anything I try will be different. I just got here."

"Right you are. What I mean is let's stay away from the obviously fancy or touristy. Let's eat where the people eat. That's the only way to savor the true cuisine of a country."

"A good way to get sick," I said.

"You're in a bad mood today. The trip wasn't easy, was it?"

"I'm all right," I said. "I'll feel better after I eat."

"Right," Martin said. "I know the place. I just noticed it this morning. It looks clean and authentic."

No one else there when we walked in and sat down, the place looked authentic all right, but I would have preferred a more familiar setting. Tablecloths had never graced the tables surrounded by chairs of the simple bentwood variety. Half-curtains hung over the windows. They had once been white but had yellowed from age and lack of care. The place reeked of the desert, making our mouths feel dusty, perhaps why Martin described it as different and authentic.

Too tired and dejected, I refrained from objecting. We sat a long time without being noticed; no menus on the tables, no one inquired what we wanted. Martin, usually incensed by anything that failed to meet his expectations, remained calm, causing me to wonder whether I was imagining the long wait. This time, Martin took the lack of service as an indication of authenticity.

"Martin, I think we are the only two people here. I think this is an abandoned building."

"Relax," he said, "the waitress will be along soon." He was very confident. "There were plenty of people here for lunch today."

"Maybe the place is closed for dinner," I said. "It may be an old Aztec custom."

"The Aztec lived farther south," Martin said. "The Indians in this part of the country always went out to dinner."

"They tore out the heart of a live waitress and ate it as an appetizer."

"No, those were the Aztecs, and they only did that for lunch."

"I see," I said.

"Ah, here she comes."

The waitress emerged from the kitchen looking very authentic—tired and sweaty and wishing for a chance to sit down and soak her feet in a bucket of Epsom salt solution.

"Que quieren?" she asked.

"El menu," Martin responded.

Her face remained blank.

"La carta," I said in an attempt to clarify.

Her face remained immobile.

"Que ay de comer?" I elaborated.

"Lo que quieran."

"La especialidad de la casa," I said.

Her expression didn't change, and she walked back to the kitchen in the same slow, deliberate pace as when she had walked to our table. She returned shortly with two bowls of stew, which we accepted uncomplainingly.

"Now this is real food," Martin said. He savored every spoonful.

Not bad but nothing to write home about, I wished I had some salad to go with it, but I remembered the stricture about eating raw food, which, along with not being able to drink tap water, was driving me up the wall. All water suspect, I only drank Pepsi Cola, the national drink of Mexico. A billboard with the familiar symbol, and proclaiming the virtues of the drink, loomed wherever I looked. Pushcart vendors and roadside stands dispensed the ubiquitous bottle. The air hot, the food salty, I had another Pepsi.

Martin looked at me disapprovingly. "There must be a native drink we can have," he said.

"There must be," I concurred and left it at that.

After the restaurant, we walked by the bay.

"There is a simpler life here," Martin said. "This harbor is still beautiful. The fishermen still go out in rowboats. It's very picturesque and still here for us to enjoy."

"And the price?"

"It's hardly costing us anything."

"Right," I said. "Do you think these fishermen who row their boats out of this harbor can afford to go on picturesque vacations?"

"You're in a bad mood. It must've been the Pepsi," Martin said slapping me on the back. "We'll save the world another day. Let's go to the disco. The *señoritas* await us."

The disco, more of a sidewalk café and an ice cream parlor combined, emanated constant rock 'n' roll. The jukebox, clearly audible throughout the neighborhood, would spout music until the late hours, a condition less than convenient for anyone trying to get a night's sleep in the hotel. A talk with Don Gregorio was to reveal that he didn't consider the noise a problem. I would also discover that despite what he had said about the hotel being completely booked for the Fiesta, my friends and I were the only guests at the moment. The hotel and the disco operated as related establishments, the disco the income-producing partner with a steady clientele of local young people, whereas the hotel had to depend on strangers, few and far between, Guaymas not a resort city. Moreover, a more modern hotel closer to the water attracted the bulk of the hotel business in town.

"There's Rick," Martin said dryly.

And indeed, I looked to see Rick in a familiar pose, one foot on a chair and leaning forward as if to impart a secret to his listeners, the middle and index fingers of his right hand holding the habitual cigarette, the grin on his face implying that he was privy to a pleasure denied to the rest of humanity, half-closed eyes indicating a transport to some other realm of existence.

"Ah, my friends, my friends," Rick exclaimed when he saw us. After a momentary pause, presumed necessary to achieve the journey back to immediate reality, he sauntered over to us, "Fate is a strange and wondrous thing. A machine of infinite complexity and one which none can escape."

He stared at me with a look intended to convey earnestness. His fleshy face at all times had a five o'clock shadow that shaving didn't remove. His large eyes drooped producing a thoroughly bovine appearance, the faculty of reason abiding behind such a façade difficult to conceive. "Ah, but I presume too much," he said taking a few effortless steps toward Martin and me, his corpulence seeming to defy gravity. The grin still on his face took on a more ambiguous meaning.

Deciphering his banter always annoying, I most often made the effort while everyone else in the group attempted to ignore his ramblings. When lucid, he exhibited admirable traits. He had a propensity for decisive action, and he fearlessly expressed his opinions. I was glad to see him back from Cuernavaca.

"And so where have you left your companion in crime?" I inquired.

Rick laughed. "We are none of us innocent. I know that much, but some of us are less guilty. That's the most we can aspire to. That's what I do and have done. And that my friend, for you are my friend, is the answer to your question and also my total defense, so it is before you now, and so will it be before our Maker when that time comes."

"Morbid, morbid, morbid," Martin said in disgust. He looked away to nobody in particular.

"On the contrary," Rick rebutted, "I am the soul of mirth. But you can't see it. But enough said. Pearls before swine! Need I say more? Our friends, Mario, spend the night in Cuernavaca. I longed for the simple life, and so here I am." With that he walked away.

Martin seethed with a rage he didn't care to conceal. "I don't know how long I can put up with this," he said. "Between Rick and Stephen I'm likely to have a mental breakdown. I'm not looking forward to a whole week of them."

"They're okay. You'll see! The fair will be fun."

"Are you here for the fair?" he asked. "But you're right; it would be a shame to miss it."

"That's right," I said.

We sat down and ordered beers, but I didn't stay long. Rick had disappeared. Not like him to retire so early, a safe bet that he wasn't back at the hotel. Not in the mood to mingle with the local patrons, mostly teenagers, scions of the well-to-do families of the town, after one beer, I went back to the hotel and tried to sleep. Music from the disco suffused the night air. Tom Jones wailing "Feelings," the favorite, lingered in the background as I, thinking of Isabel, gradually drifted into slumber.

13

The next day, Martin and I ran into Stephen and Margaret at the top of the landing. They were just returning from Cuernavaca.

"Where's Laura?" Martin asked, ready to appoint himself wagon master.

"She's still downstairs, a little shook up about the accident," Margaret said.

"What accident?" Martin inquired but was ignored.

"I'll go get her," Margaret continued.

"I'll go," I said.

"I can help her just as well," Margaret insisted.

"Let Mario do it," Stephen chimed in.

"What accident?" Martin again asked.

"Someone fell off the train," Stephen said.

"Oh, well, those things happen," Martin declared.

Down in the courtyard I tried to console Laura, who, still shaken, was sitting on one of the metal chairs. "Are you all right?" I asked.

"Yes," she said. "The tiles are pretty," she added indicating the paved floor.

"Yes," I said, "they remind me of my childhood."

"Do they?" she remarked absent-mindedly.

"I'm sorry you had to see an accident," I said.

"Yeah," she said, "me too. It was an old man. He must have been trying to get from one car to another. Why did you come down?"

"In case you needed help, and Margaret and Stephen seemed involved with each other."

"I guess she's trying hard."

"I suppose hard work makes people feel like they earned something."

"I suppose it does," she said. "We'll just have to stay out of their way."

"We'll manage. Let me take your pack up."

"I can do it," she said. So she carried her own pack up the stairs.

"Why don't we look around town?" I suggested once everybody's luggage had been deposited in the rooms. Martin and Rick had gone off to explore a pool hall they had spied the night before.

"Why don't the two of you go?" Margaret said. "Stephen and I thought we'd hang out here awhile."

"Fine," I said, looking at Laura for her assent.

We walked out to the street to explore the town that curled itself around the bay. We watched pelicans fish. Never before having seen one in the flesh, the fact that their elastic beak pouch bulged only when they scooped surprised me. In the distance, the signs of industry were apparent and, as always, ominously ugly. There were large ships anchored out in the bay, but the downtown waterfront seemed only to cater to fishing boats and other small crafts.

For a while we watched a group of urchins dive off the jetty. Then we walked on until we arrived at the square with the obligatory church at one end.

"It's always the same," I said. "It's funny, in Hispanic places there is always a square with a church. In New England towns there is always a green with a gazebo."

"How sociological you sound."

"It's just talk," I said. "I wish Isabel were here already."

"Oh, is she coming down?"

"She said she might."

"Well, we'll all be glad to see her," she said in an unconvincing voice.

14

The next morning, we all went to El Gallito for breakfast. Having slept late, lunch was being served when we got there. The waitress thought our orders humorous, confirming for her that Americans were indeed odd. But perhaps she only thought us young, and the young everywhere prone to the unusual.

Americans, however, unexplainably seemed to preserve their oddness beyond youth. Just the day before everyone on the street had stopped to observe a visiting American couple. The husband slowly drove their camper while the wife, for some indecipherable reason, walked in front of it. Though the camper was indeed an unusual vehicle in Guaymas, that was not what induced the natives to stop to scrutinize the visitors. Rather, the attention focused on the woman's look and attire—sandals, short-shorts, halter top, and sunglasses. Her blond curls lifted to the top of her head reminded the onlookers of a volcanic eruption.

How much flesh she exhibited on the streets of a foreign city became the talk of the town. Even we, her fellow citizens, now having breakfast at lunchtime, were amused, if not scandalized, by the exhibit of an embarrassing national quirk. Of course, if Isabel had been with us, she would have more than compensated for the embarrassing spectacle of the woman in the street.

Thankfully, those odd Americans were nowhere in sight at the moment. From the veranda of El Gallito, we viewed the spectators beginning to line the street to wait for the parade. Rather, it would be more a procession than a parade, the festival traditionally having a distinctly religious overtone.

"There they come," Margaret almost shouted pointing toward the end of the street where a military band, followed by a cavalry squadron, had turned the corner and had paused to adjust formation.

"Here the military is ahead of everything," Rick said.

"Don't let that fool you," Laura said.

"That's the one thing that's bothered me on this trip," I said. "The military seems to be the same as the police."

"That's because the police are so corrupt they don't do their job properly."

"Is that the reason?"

Rick had limited himself to alcohol during the trip, fearing that as an American, he was unfairly under police surveillance. Stephen, for his part, had decided to ascribe Rick's fear merely to paranoia having little to do with reality, assuming of course that reality had a common base for the rest of the group and perhaps for humanity in general.

"Maybe, maybe not. What is it to us? We'll be back home soon enough."

"Back home they do it secretly. We might all be on an FBI list."

"Yeah? What are you listed for?"

"I'm listed for drinking Mexican beer," Stephen said.

"Is that all?"

"Isn't that enough?"

After the military band and cavalry squadron went by, a pause ensued before the street filled again with a group of drummers dressed in Aztec costumes. They ushered in the central figure, Montezuma as a tragic hero, who proceeded to dance about the street as regally as possible. Directly behind him marched the villain, the Spanish conquistador.

"And who is that supposed to be?" Margaret asked.

"That's Cortez," I said, "the bad guy."

"Everyone here speaks Spanish, but the Spanish were the bad guys?"

"Well, we speak English and our revolution was against the English."

"That's not the same," Laura said. "After all, it wasn't the Iroquois who revolted against the English."

"You mean Thomas Jefferson wasn't a Cherokee?"

"Neither was Washington."

"No, only Alexander Hamilton was a native. That's why he was shot by Aaron Burr."

"I didn't know that," Margaret said with a straight face, no one sure whether she was joking or whether she really believed Hamilton had been a Native American.

"Oh, look, who's that?" Laura inquired pointing to another figure in Aztec costume who cavorted about as if casting a spell over Cortez. This character, much more ornate than the others, wore an elaborated mask half white and half black.

"He must be another Aztec saint," Stephen said.

"Of course," Rick exclaimed, "just what I expected. This is marvelous. Everything is getting to me."

"Better late than never," Stephen said.

After the military and historical scenes went by the parade took on a religious tone, naturally enough culminating at the square in front of the church. The brown statue of the Virgin of Guadalupe came by.

"Wow, is that a black Virgin Mary?" Laura asked addressing no one in particular.

"Well, she's not quite black," Stephen said. "She's more of a redskin."

"You mean an Indian, don't you?"

"He means a Native American."

"An Aztec Virgin?"

"We should go down to the square and see what's happening there," Margaret suggested.

"One more beer then we'll go," Stephen said.

"I've had enough," I said.

"Enough beer or enough festival?"

"Enough beer," Margaret said. "I think you all had enough."

"And the day is young," Rick said.

Rick and Stephen each had another beer, then we all went down to the square where a band on each side competed for the crowd, a needless effort since so many people filled the square that the crowd overflowed into the side streets.

"Why don't we go into the church and see what's going on in there?"

"The church is already full," I said.

"Do they close the doors when it's full?"

"No, but it'll be hard to get in. Not worth the trouble."

In the evening, fireworks lit up the sky. All the while, rides, food concessions, and gambling booths, like the ones I recalled from my childhood, continued to hold the crowd.

15

On the second day of the festival, I suddenly came down with a fever, and right away I knew why. I wasn't supposed to drink the water or eat anything uncooked. I had been careful about the water, but I had eaten lettuce at a luncheonette. The next day, the fever weakened me so much I couldn't move. I stayed in bed and hallucinated. I saw below the surface of every object. Everything I gazed at was composed of interlocking straight lines. The revelation mesmerized me, and I proceeded to look at one object after another to see how the whole world was connected. My body also became a series of straight lines merging with everything else in the room. I blended with the physical surroundings. I wondered whether this fluidity was a manifestation of my death. I only regretted not having waited for Isabel to arrive before I died. I heard a muzzled voice in the room, and I concentrated to identify it. Finally I heard Laura say, "You need a doctor."

She later told me that I refused to see a doctor, but I didn't remember saying anything, only seeing her merge with everything in the room. She also had become a series of straight lines. Laura brought me food and kept me well supplied with aspirins. When the fever reached a peak, she tried cooling me down with rubbing alcohol. When that wasn't enough, she wrapped me in wet towels. The next day she was there again. The whole group came to the door, but she kept them from entering the room. They dropped by several times a day and waved at me, and I knew they were my friends. Still, I longed for Isabel to come down for me to get well and be happy.

"You're one hell of a nurse," I said to Laura.

"I've had better patients."

"I'll be all right."

"I suppose you will," she said, "but you're taking a chance."

"That's what life is, isn't it?"

"Illness makes you philosophical."

"Isabel is not going to come down, is she?"

"I don't know," she said.

"I don't either," I said staring at the ceiling.

By the third day I felt better though still weak and unable to eat much. I had a craving for fruit, but nothing tasted right. Martin brought me an apple pie from the supermarket, but the crust was made with lard, and I couldn't stand it.

On the fourth day, I was able to go downstairs. A postcard from

Isabel awaited me at the front desk. She was sorry, but she wouldn't be able to meet me. I stared at the card for a long time, then I went out to sit in the patio. In the past, Isabel would have pursued me to the ends of the earth. A year before, I could have gone to Antarctica, and she would have followed. I recognized that I had made mistakes, but there was no way to get through life without mistakes. I was willing to atone for mine if she would only give me another chance.

Or perhaps she had never loved me, and I had imagined her attachment. I wondered whether my imagination had such scope, or whether, psychologically impaired, I was unable to tell the difference between reality and fantasy. I had to pull myself together and not think nonsense or give her more power than in reality was possible for her to wield. I tried to convince myself that she was just as trapped by Fate and probably suffering more than I.

The patio sparkled in the morning sunlight, but I could only stare at the stone floor. I watched an ant crawl over what must have seemed to it an endless expanse. Alone, it carted something three or four times its own size. I wondered if it knew where it was or whether it had lost its way. No access to the ground through the stone and cement of the courtyard was visible. No other ants in sight, it continued its journey as if it knew exactly where it was going, the possibility or impossibility of the task beyond its concern.

"I'm going home," I announced to my friends when they came down to join me.

"No need to do that, Mario," Martin said. "By tomorrow you'll be as good as new. You'll see."

"Nah," I said. "I have to go."

"You sure? I thought I'd go down to Mexico City and then to the Yucatan."

"Don't worry," I said. "I can make it on my own."

"Actually, I was thinking of going home also," Stephen said surprising everyone, especially Margaret. "I'll see that Mario gets home in one piece," he continued, the usual smirk on his face.

"So, just Martin and I will escort the ladies down to the pyramids," Rick said. He grinned as he concluded that in some inexplicable way he had beaten Stephen. All he had to do now was figure out how he had done it.

Stephen and I left the next day, by bus this time, for San Diego, from where we flew back to New York.

16

Renwick Street became a desolate place for me. I telephoned Isabel one more time.

"I'm coming out to see you again," I said.

"Please don't," she said.

"I have to."

"I won't be here," she answered. "I'm going to Arizona."

"I'll meet you in Arizona," I said.

"I'm going with Larry Lessing."

After a pause I asked, "Is it serious?"

"Don't ask me that. It's always serious."

"Okay," I said.

After I hung up, I stared out the window for a long time. Not much to look at on the street, the neighborhood desolate, the warehouses and factories closed for the weekend. A taxi pulled up, and a long-legged young woman, Sunflower Kelly, one of the girls who lived on the fifth floor, scrambled out. I noticed that beneath all the makeup lurked a pretty face. She stood on the sidewalk balancing herself on her spike heels and shouted up to her roommate to come down because a couple of customers waited in the taxi.

At the fifth-floor window, her friend didn't understand the message. Sunflower, about to shout again, hesitated when she noticed me. Instead, in a show of unnecessary delicacy, she gestured to her colleague to come down. In a few minutes, Sunflower's roommate emerged wearing the tightest miniskirt I had ever seen. Both women climbed into the taxi, and I watched it drive down the street until it turned the corner. When I got tired of looking at the empty street, I walked across the room to my desk, and for a while, I gazed at the photograph of Isabel.

Margarita

*D*EMONS CAME OUT of their hiding place to hound me. I turned to Margarita for help.

"Take me out to dinner," she said.

"Shall we take your husband too?"

"Baby, that's up to you!"

We went to a Cuban restaurant, ate a great deal of *ropa vieja* and rice, and drank much sangria; afterward, I took her home. I watched her undress, her long black hair falling all the way to the small of her back. Then long slender legs wrapped around mine, pulling me in, heaving under me, and I driving flesh into flesh, trying to make the feeling in my groins exorcise the demons that possessed me. Afterward, I told her a dream I had a few nights before. "A gang broke into my apartment wanting me to let them live there. They were a desperate-looking bunch."

"And did you let them in?"

"I was frightened. I told them to get out."

"And then?"

"They grumbled as they slowly began to move out. Some of them reached for books and figurines that were on a shelf. I had a knife in my hand and threw it at the one trying to steal the book. It hit him on the wrist."

"Wow, that must have made them mad."

"But just then, a woman walked in who told them she would find them another place to live. That quieted them and they left."

"Who was the woman?"

"I don't know," I said. "She looked a little like you."

"I saved you. You read lots of books, but books don't say everything."

The doorbell rang. The sound startled me, always the possibility of Margarita's husband changing his mind about letting her work me for as much as he could get. Or rather, had a change of heart, I doubted that he had any mind left; probably whatever remained was beyond repair.

"It's my mother with Sammy," Margarita said, putting her hand on my shoulder.

"What time is it?"

"It's eleven. What am I going to do? I don't want her to know you're here."

"Don't tell her."

"She'll know someone's here."

She put on her nightgown and went to the door. I waited in the bedroom. It reminded me of my mother's. In addition to the bed, there was a dresser with a mirror, a matching bureau and two night tables, all poorly constructed and veneered in dark brown, bought on time in a store that sported a sign, *"Aquí se habla Español,"* but which meant, "Here we'll charge you ten times as much."

The old lady sat very straight at the edge of the sofa, as if relaxing would have implied approval of her daughter's behavior. She didn't sit in the armchair but on the sofa with the plastic slipcover, sat up straight, at the edge, in an effort to show discomfort. She didn't look up into the mirror hanging on the wall across from her. Perhaps she had one just like it, a leopard crouching in one corner. She stared into the darkened hallway that led to the door. Occasionally, searching for evidence that her words of opprobrium received proper attention, she glared at Margarita.

She scolded in generalities, leaving it up to Margarita to apply them to herself. She delivered her words with the certainty that such things had to be said. The words came wrapped in understanding, chastisement without rancor, without hope of immediate result and with full trust in God's mercy and reason. That was the strength and the weakness of her people. She did not expect indifference from a deity, and much less did she expect cruelty.

I heard the footsteps on the worn linoleum, then the metallic sound of the lock as Margarita opened the door to let her mother out. I heard Margarita's footsteps coming back down the hallway. She called her son to come into the bedroom, and he followed her.

"Hello Sammy," I said.

The boy, small boned and frail, his eyes large like his father's, looking at the floor, stood at the foot of the bed and remained silent. Margarita picked the child up and holding him sat on the bed.

"Say hello to Mario," she said to the child. Sammy stared at the wall. "Talk to Mario," she solicitously urged. "He's going to take us away from here."

I got out of the bed and began to dress.

"You are going to take us away, right?"

"Where would I take you?" I asked, pulling up my zipper and buckling my belt. "And what about your husband?"

"He doesn't care now."

"That's because he thinks you're getting money out of me, and he needs money. He might take a different view if suddenly you weren't around to prop him up." I buttoned my shirt and began to knot my tie, but remembering the time and place, I slipped it off and stuffed it in my pocket.

"Another woman would be less trouble to you. Why do you come to me?"

"I don't know," I said.

"You know," she insisted.

"Maybe I do," I conceded.

Once I stepped out of the apartment, the dirty walls, the cracked plaster, and the smell of urine assaulted me. Out in the street, people sat drinking, making music, playing dominoes. Margarita's image floated before me.

Street urchins having opened a hydrant at the end of the block, the garbage floated on the water down to the corner to clog the sewer. I quickened my pace. As I approached, I signaled the boys at the hydrant to keep the water down. They waited, and when I got within range, they let me have it. They dropped the can and ran as the water cascaded down on me.

Going Home

Oranges

WHEN I WAS a child, my mother would cut a hole on top of an orange, and I would squeeze the orange and suck out the juice. It got all over my face, and when it dried, my face felt sticky. On Sundays, when we came out of church, there was always a pushcart vendor in the square selling oranges and orange juice. He peeled the oranges with a knife, so that the rind came off in one long strand. I was fascinated by that achievement. I couldn't wait to grow up and be able to peel an orange in one continuous strip.

I watched my grandfather plow the field on the side of the hill, and I marveled how at the end of the row he made the ox turn around and plow in the opposite direction. That seemed like magic to me. I wanted to do it also, but I wasn't old enough yet to hold the plow. When I was eight years old, my family moved to New York. I never saw anybody plow with an ox again. I never again saw anybody peel an orange in one continuous strip with a knife.

My grandfather seemed like a tall man to me, but actually he wasn't tall at all. But I didn't see him for a long time after we came to New York, and I remembered him the way he seemed to me when I was a child. He wore leather leggings that buckled on. They were meant for riding. He was a great one for horses.

"You're going to die with your boots on," my father said to him once.

Grandfather turned to another man standing with them. "So you hear how my own son speaks to me?"

Grandfather smiled as he said that—a smile that he had, my father also, a smile that they put on when they were pleased with themselves. I looked at Grandfather's feet and saw that he wasn't wearing boots. I thought that maybe my father meant that Grandfather would die with his leggings on. From the look on Grandfather's face, I concluded that

197

dying fully clothed was something good, though I couldn't imagine why. Dead is dead, I thought, boots or no boots.

Down by the edge of Grandfather's land, a stream cascaded into a little waterfall—about six feet or so. At the bottom of the fall, the stream widened into a small pool, a good place to shower in those days of no indoor plumbing. Just on the other side of the stream flourished a grapefruit orchard. Grandfather and I went down to the stream, climbed the bluff over the waterfall, and he crawled under the barbwire.

"You stay here," he said. "You'll be the catcher."

I watched him climb up a tree. He reached out for the grapefruits and then tossed them to me. I peered anxiously into the brush thinking that the American who owned that land would appear any minute and catch us red-handed. After he had picked several grapefruits, he climbed down, crawled back under the barbwire, and booty in hand, we started back for the house. My anxiety persisted until we rounded a bend in the trail.

"Stealing is a sin," I said, remembering my mother's admonitions.

"It surely is," he answered.

"We'll go to hell, you and I," I said.

"Nonsense," he said, "two upstanding fellows like us; we're writ in the book of the chosen."

"What book is that?" I asked. I thought that maybe it was a book that one had to sign; maybe they kept it in the church or in the rectory. I didn't remember having signed any such book. Of course, maybe somebody had signed for me, and I didn't know anything about it; maybe they signed your name at baptism or confirmation. I didn't know.

"You know the gospel says, 'Many are the called, but few are the chosen. Not all those who cry Lord! Lord! shall be saved.'" Grandfather explained to me. "You see, it doesn't matter what you do in this world because the chosen are already picked out, and we're in."

That sounded somewhat heretical to me, but it made sense. After all, that's what the gospel said. "Even so," I said, "it's still a sin to steal."

"We didn't steal anything," Grandfather said. "We're only nationalizing these grapefruit. If God wanted a gringo to have these grapefruits, He would have put the trees in North America."

Grandfather's logic was implacable. I had yet to learn that morality, religion, and logic had very little in common, and the three were rarely on speaking terms. I could never go by the behavior of adults on these matters. They were often contradictory and confusing. Good people were supposed to go to church on Sundays, but my grandfather and my uncles never did. My father attended sometimes. Only women in my family went to church regularly.

I heard Grandfather many times say that religion was for women. If so, it certainly wasn't for me. Nevertheless, my mother dragged me to church every Sunday. I tried to appeal to my father, but it was no use. "Leave the boy home," he said once. "He's too young yet." My mother flew into a rage, and my father never mentioned it again. Direct confrontation was not his style. My mother had a temper, which made it seem as if she were confronting, but actually she was only losing control of herself, something she never considered a desirable trait. Consequently, she never condoned the expression of anger in anyone else.

The men were not fazed, however, by my mother's insistence on my strict religious upbringing. They launched a quiet counteratack that seemed at times a tug of war for my soul, my mother on one side representing the church, which claimed to represent God; and my paternal male relatives on the other, representing the world, which they claimed was a truer representation of God, and if it wasn't, all the worse for Him.

Grandfather never missed a chance to say something disparaging about priests. His most common assertion, which made my mother livid, was that our parish priest was a drunkard and a womanizer.

"Do you know how much wine is delivered to the rectory every month?"

How much? I wondered, but he never said.

"I don't want to hear that kind of talk in front of my child," my mother would say as she ushered me out of the room.

From the kitchen, I heard voices dimly saying something about celibacy and Grandfather laughing derisively. Later, I asked my mother, "Is Grandpa going to hell?"

"Don't say such things," she snapped.

"Isn't he sinful?"

"God will forgive him," she said without conviction.

But the old man kept an oil lamp burning in front of an icon; it burned twenty-four hours a day. I'm sure he prayed in front of that icon when no one was watching or maybe only in the presence of Julia, my grandmother.

"Why do you burn oil?" I asked him once.

"I made a promise to the Virgin," he said. "I'm a man of my word."

"What promise?"

"A promise," he said, and I knew to stop asking him.

I asked my mother.

"That's between your grandfather and the Virgin," she answered.

The burning oil lamp fascinated me, and I wondered what possible good it could do for my grandfather. Why would such an irreligious man promise the Virgin to keep a lamp perpetually burning? Perhaps we had been in similar situations. One night, I was seized with the certainty that I would die before the sun came up. I broke out into a sweat. I tried to reason with myself: I'm perfectly healthy; there's no cause why I would die tonight of all nights. I couldn't think of any sins that would keep me from entering heaven if I did indeed die, but that was no comfort at all. I didn't want to die. But the more I longed for life the more certain I was that I would die. I knew that if I dozed off, I wouldn't wake up in this world, but the task of keeping my eyes open till daybreak was beyond my powers. I had to make some other arrangement. I had to make a deal with God, whom I took for a wheeler-dealer.

Yes, of course, a deal would work! I had heard a missionary once describe how, before he became a servant of God, he had been shipwrecked. The sea whirled about him as he clung to some wreckage. "Lord," he cried, "if you spare my life, I will serve you always." And God heard him. Ever since that day, the man roamed the world preaching the Word.

I had to come up with a better deal than that, one that was acceptable to God but would allow me some leeway. I certainly didn't want to be a missionary or anything remotely similar. I thought of giving up ice cream. That would be a great sacrifice that God would certainly appreciate. I reconsidered; a life without ice cream was not a life. I had to give up something dear enough to impress God but not so dear that the lack of it would be unbearable. Chewing gum! That was perfect. I had no doubt that I could live without chewing gun, something I loved dearly. "God," I said, "if you spare me now, I'll never chew gum again." I figured that would do it.

I didn't expect God to acknowledge the deal with any spectacular display of thunder or earth quaking. It was better this way, quiet and dignified. I decided to sleep, but in a little while it occurred to me that I had not specified how long I should live. After all, I might die the next week, and it would not be a breach of contract on God's part. I had to add another clause. What would be a reasonable amount of time for which to ask a guarantee? One hundred and fifty years would be nice, but it seemed exorbitant. God would never go for that. I didn't want to take advantage of Him. After all, He might get angry and call the whole thing off. I decided on fifty years as an equitable figure. And with that I went to sleep.

Now, in relation to my grandfather's promise I wondered whether he had undergone some great fear from which the Virgin had delivered him. There were problems with that supposition. I couldn't imagine Grandfather being afraid of anything, not even death. A man who would die with his boots on is a fearless man. Why would he have the Virgin intercede for him? Why didn't he deal with God directly,

Man to man? Why involve a woman? It wasn't like Grandfather to do business that way. I was thoroughly confused.

I was preoccupied with the image of my grandfather, but I was not close to him. I don't know whether he was close to anybody except my grandmother. He wasn't close to his offspring, and they in turn don't know how to be close to theirs.

Grandfather was always, in the back of my mind, the ideal man in the old tradition, *macho completo* as they used to say when I was a boy. His sons were in awe of him. His wife worshipped him, or so it seemed. Grandmother served dinner at the same time every day. We sat around the table. Grandfather's chair was empty, but his place was set. She dished out his portion as if he were present, then she covered his plate. Once, my mother suggested that the food would stay warmer if it was left in the pot. "The head of household gets served first, always," Grandmother snapped. There was nothing further to be said. Mother never saw things that way. That was only one of the matters about which she and Grandmother never agreed.

Grandmother disapproved of the way my parents were raising me. She believed that they were spoiling me. She was especially critical of my mother's attitude, with the result that Mother was always nervous in her presence. I was a finicky eater, and my mother would try as hard as she could to find things I liked to eat. If I didn't like what everyone else was eating, she would cook something just for me. Grandmother disapproved of that. She thought I should be forced to eat whatever was set on the table. Chicken was my nemesis. I hated chicken unless it was so well cooked that it could pass for something else.

One day, I wouldn't eat the chicken. I sat in front of the plate for what seemed hours, my mother urging me to eat, Grandmother skulking about in the background. My mother wasn't usually so persistent, but Grandmother's presence intimidated her. Finally, she took out a strap and threatened me. "I don't like chicken," I insisted between sobs. She hit me with the strap twice. In her discomfiture, she inadvertently used the buckle end of the strap.

She was immediately overcome with remorse and clutched me

to her breast kissing me and proclaiming she was sorry. For days the buckle marks remained on my thigh. Every day she would inspect them and with tears in her eyes apologize. She still remembers that incident with regret. My mother is very forgiving and eventually forgave my grandmother for that and for everything else.

The old lady did not, however, take my forgiveness to her grave but merely my indifference. I was in my teens when, on a visit to New York, she was killed in a traffic accident. When I heard the news, I felt nothing and that puzzled me. I expected to be automatically overwhelmed by grief on such an occasion. I tried to feel something, but all that emerged was an artificial sense of excitement. Even that didn't last long. Having manufactured it out of a sense of duty, I had not the will or, consequently, the energy to maintain it. At the funeral, my cousins were all crying. Those who had been raised by my grandparents were rather hysterical. Not wanting them to think I was hard-hearted, I tried to disguise my lack of sorrow.

I looked into the coffin, and I saw a waxen old woman. She was a stranger to me. I knew less about her than about a casual acquaintance, and yet she was my grandmother. I must have spent a considerable amount of time in her presence, but she never entered my imagination. Who was this woman?

I didn't remember her ever saying anything kind to me. My most vivid recollection of her was her admonishing me not to crawl under the house after the dogs, possibly infested with fleas. Well, that was kind enough; she didn't want me to get bitten by the fleas. But did she have to tell me in that tone? It is very likely that she was not a happy woman. As a child, that was beyond my ken. I couldn't imagine an adult with so much power having an unhappy life.

Grandfather outlived her by twelve years. I seldom saw him during that time. He spent most of it in Puerto Rico. After a long stretch, I saw him again when he came to New York. He didn't look any older, but I had grown some, and he no longer towered over me. We embraced, and I was amazed at the power of his arms. The old man was still strong. He still drank his share of rum, but he had acquired prayer as a form of expression. One day, I inadvertently came upon him as he knelt, rosary in hand, before an icon. I was embarrassed to see him in that position. He was oblivious of my presence, as if such behavior had been customary all of his life. I quickly averted my eyes and walked away.

A few days later he caused a disturbance at a wedding. A man took offense at the attention my grandfather was paying to his wife. The old man had to be rescued from the resulting scuffle. "He has spunk in him yet," my uncles grinned. My mother was appalled: "At his age! Shameful!" I was amused and a little proud that I was a descendant of such a man.

I didn't see the old man during his final illness. I was but vaguely aware that he still existed. He had long ceased to be a real person to me, had been apotheosized, absorbed into a mythology of ideal manhood; he lived with Horatio, Cincinnatus, Roland, and William Tell. The idea would not have occurred to me that I was obliged to visit any such personages. Their apotheosis would have kept them from noticing me.

When I heard of my grandfather's death, I was not grieved, but my lack of sorrow did not surprise me. I didn't try to hide it. I wasn't ashamed of it. Perhaps because I loved my grandfather, even from a distance, as I had not loved my grandmother. There wasn't as much crying at Grandfather's funeral as there had been at Grandmother's. His death did not shock anybody. He was old and had been ill for a while. He wasn't one to go without a fight, and he hung in for a long time. I wondered whether anybody, in those last hours, had thought of fitting him in his boots.

The funeral afforded me an opportunity to see many relatives I had not seen for a while. I had recently married, and this was the first time that many of them were meeting my wife. Distant cousins whom I had not seen for ten years gave me their addresses and begged me to come visit them. I could see the sincerity in their faces.

Cousin Lilian chided me for not keeping in touch. Her round face and large eyes were still as beautiful as in her childhood. Although she was already the mother of three, she still radiated innocence.

She had married as soon as she graduated from high school. She squeezed my arm, and I remembered how when children we had loved each other. We had grown up together, practically in the same house. We would get married when we grew up, I thought. Then in our adolescence a terrible and bewildering change occurred. I lost her; other boys were more interesting to her. She married someone else.

"Mario and I used to be so close when we were children, then we grew apart," she said to my wife. "We must stay in touch now. We have to make the effort."

Cousin Manuel had memories too. "You remember the two of us and Papo, we used to go crabbing in Mucarabones?"

Papo? Who was Papo? I had no memory. Was I becoming senile while still in my twenties?

"Those were the good old days," he assured me. He meant it. His face beamed with the joy of those long gone days. I had no memory of crabbing. I was afraid of crabs when I was a child, afraid of the claws that could grab me and tear my fingers off.

"Papo?" I questioned.

"Yes, Papo, our cousin, Julio's son."

Ah, yes, a dark shadowy figure emerged from the past, but I could not distinguish his face or anything else about his character or his relationship to me. I was astounded by the vivid memories Manuel had of our childhood together. I had but few.

I remembered cutting branches from some bushes, making bows and arrows, then stalking the dogs. We pretended they were wild tigers, but the dogs didn't like the game. They ran under the house knowing we were forbidden to follow them there, where they stayed until we got tired of waiting for them to come out. We went up the road to shoot our arrows at the neighbor's chickens.

As a teenager bent on raising hell, Manuel got into trouble. He joined the marines to avoid prison. While I was in college getting a degree, he was in Vietnam getting a Purple Heart and a limp.

"They all love you," my wife said to me on our way home. "They look up to you."

In my youth, I had merely wanted to be one of them.

In a recent talk with my mother, I mentioned my paternal grandfather. There were things about him that were still unclear to me. He and Grandmother had never married; not one of their children bore his name. The minute I broached the subject my mother let out a stream of vituperations against my grandfather, and immediately she asked God's forgiveness for speaking that way about the dead.

"I don't know how your grandmother put up with it. She had to work hard to bring up those children. God forgive me, but it's the truth; that man was just trouble."

That was news to me.

"And the women, all the other women, how Julia put up with that, I don't know."

"Why didn't they marry?"

"He was married to someone else, but she couldn't bear children. She was a sickly woman, but she lived a long time. All your uncles were grown up by the time she passed away."

"Why didn't he marry Grandmother then?"

"Your grandfather was a shameless man. But with age, he stuck to your grandmother."

There wasn't any more to be said about the matter. His sons took after him. I hadn't seen my father for months. He wouldn't accept my invitations, and he never tendered any of his own. We saw each other by chance, when we visited other relatives. He was always cordial but distant.

My mother sat across from me in the armchair. Above the chair, on the pale yellow wall, hung one of my brother's watercolor paintings, a woman in an eighteenth-century costume. The winter light filtered into the room through the sheer curtains. My sister, watering can in hand, came in to water the plants. "Don't mind me," she said. "I'm like the hired help around here."

"I don't know what I would do without my children," Mother said. "They're all I have left. I was happy with your father once."

I don't remember them ever being happy together except when I was very young. There was always trouble and tension in the house, but my mother had constructed a past full of happiness. I don't know whether I exaggerated my memories of strife or whether she minimized hers.

"If you were so happy, what do you think went wrong?" I asked.

"I don't know. That's the way men are, but women always have their children as compensation."

My wife and I went to Puerto Rico soon after our wedding, my first trip back to the island since leaving twenty years before. The cities had changed, but the mountains were still the same. I was disappointed to see the pushcart vendors who sold oranges. They didn't peel the oranges with a knife but had a mechanical peeler, like a small lathe, that did the job very quickly and efficiently. It required no skill to turn the crank; anyone could do it, even a youngster.

We drove up from Mayaguez following the contour of the mountains. The scenery reminded me of going to visit my grandparents when I was a child. My wife, a native New Yorker, had never before been in a tropical forest. We stopped several times to examine the foliage. Plantain trees and orange trees grew wild.

"Are those really oranges?"

"Of course they are," I said. "Let me pick one for you."

"They must belong to someone."

"Nah," I said. "They grow all over the place." I descended the slope a short distance until an overhanging branch came within reach. I picked one of the oranges. "Here you are," I said handing her the prize.

Back in the car, she started to peel it. "How do you know it's not poisonous?" she asked.

"It's just an orange," I said.

She put it to her lips and quickly turned away, an expression of disgust on her face. "Ugh, it's bitter."

"Let me see." I tasted it also. Indeed, it tasted more like a lemon than an orange. "Well, so much for wild oranges," I said.

We chucked it out, and it rolled down the slope to join its fallen brethren.

www.ingramcontent.com/pod-product-compliance
Lightning Source LLC
Chambersburg PA
CBHW050530260626
47157CB00004B/1541